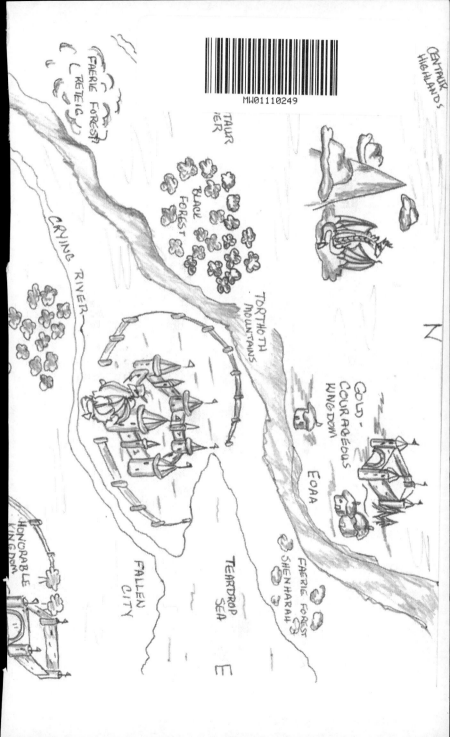

The Secret of Avonoa

Enjoy the
adventure!

Heidi

H. R. B. Collotzi

ISBN: 1499758537
ISBN 13: 9781499758535
Library of Congress Control Number: 2014910170
CreateSpace Independent Publishing Platform
North Charleston, South Carolina

www.avonoa.com

For Jason
My love, My heart
Forever

Contents

Contents

I

Failure

"You failed? AGAIN!?" The young gray dragon's voice rose with each word. He let out a plaintive growl while gouging all four claws into the rock underneath as if he might find some escape through them. "By The One, Dak! This makes FOUR times!" he moaned, then finally turned one of his protruding eyes back to his friend.

Dak bared his fangs. "Do you think I enjoy this, Tog?"

"I'm beginning to wonder!" Tog turned to stomp past the other dragons waiting to see if their young ones and friends had passed. "The Krusible is the most important test in a young dragon's life!" he said over his shoulder.

"I know." Dak responded to the short spikes running down his friend's back. Although they were both the same age, Tog had a tendency to treat Dak like a youngling.

"Most dragons don't take the Krusible more than twice."

"I know."

"Five times is unheard of!"

"I know."

"All you have to do is remain silent!"

"I know!" Dak yelled.

Tog turned to face his friend. "You'll never get away from the Rock Clouds if you don't pass!"

"I'll find a way," Dak grumbled.

Tog shook his head. "You say that as if there aren't dozens of specially trained dragons guarding our entire ruck both sun and moon cycle." Dak rolled one shoulder as if pushing off a pest and turned away. As both dragons unfurled their wings preparing to spring into the air, Tog gave Dak a sidelong glare. "What happened this time?"

"Milah," Dak answered simply, then launched himself free of the rock.

"Oh no," Tog moaned again while he followed his friend to the sky. "Show me when we land."

As they pumped their wings, Dak turned to scan the Krusible. It was a spacious round depression on the edge of the Inner Mountain seeming as if a giant had lovingly sculpted it out of the side of the rocky crags. While the Krusible itself was smooth enough for hatchlings to slide around when the first winter snows and ice came, the outside edges were hedged with jagged boulders. The ringed stone bowl was naturally secluded – perfect for the test.

On the day of the Krusible, the adult dragons in charge, usually male, would test the young dragons from sunup to sundown. The young dragons knew not to utter a single word, no matter what test of their wills the adult dragons imposed. The adult testers would attempt every means they could devise – short only of death – to compel the young ones to speak. May the gods help you if you fell asleep! There was no end to the taunts and abuses of their testers who continued with the single motive to make the young ones speak.

From the air, Dak eyed the handful of young dragons still lying unmoving in the stone bowl of the Krusible, with two large brown dragons watching over them. Milah and Mitashio. The brothers had recently been put in charge of testing the young dragons. Milah caught Dak's distant gaze and tossed him an evil half-grin before whispering something to his brother. The two bellowed with laughter as Dak tore his eyes away.

"I hate those two." Dak said just loud enough for Tog to hear. He rolled his shoulder again.

The two dragons flew around the Rock Clouds – large detached rocks and mountains which floated around the towering Inner Mountain with the Krusible. Some of the floating rocks were smaller than a horse, but many of them were mountains in their own right, as large as the Torthoth Mountains in the distance, with caves mottling the sides able to house dozens of dragons in each. The Rock Clouds swam through the air at all times while keeping an invisible anchor to the largest of them all - the Inner Mountain. The Inner Mountain was the only one attached at its base to the earth, yet it reached so high that only the most determined dragons could ascend to the top.

The land at the base of the Inner Mountain remained sparse of brush and tree even in the summer season. As the Rock Clouds passed over, they often deprived the vegetation beneath of sunlight for days at a time, so only the hardiest of plants survived. A few caves dotted the base of the Inner Mountain, but those were reserved for The Watch.

As they flew around the edge of a mountain, Dak caught the faint groan of forewarning just in time to see a large rock that matched him in size drift directly in front of him. He beat his wings to rise above it, then pressed on the rock with all four claws, pushing it away to change its course. He didn't look at his friend, but could feel Tog's eyes rolling at his playful behavior. Secretly, Dak hoped the rock would knock some little fledgling off their course.

The weakening winter sun warming his back couldn't lift Dak's spirit. Although the harsh cold of winter never reached its fingers completely into the Rock Clouds where they lived, the landscape still took on a shadow of the barren world beneath. Through the warm seasons, the floating mountains grew lush with greenery and trickled with streams and waterfalls, but winter had spread among them early this year. The lakes froze in their valley homes. The leaves departed the trees. Even the cold stone bowl of the Krusible had tried to strangle the fire in Dak's belly.

Dak hoped taking the Krusible on the shortest sun cycle of the year would have given him an advantage. He swatted at an icicle that dribbled from the remnants of a waterfall as Tog watched through one narrowed eye. The two friends flew in silence, their mutual frustration stewing. As their claws tramped onto the mouth of the cave where Dak lived with his father, Tusten, neither dragon wanted to bring up the subject again.

But Tog forced it out before Dak could get very far in the cave. "Well?" he demanded of the two horns on the back of the black dragon's head.

Once inside, Dak sighed, then twisted his long neck around to face Tog crowding the entrance. Putting his nostrils only inches from his friend's, he brought the memory of his test to the front of his mind. Concentrating on the scene, he breathed hot air and the memory into Tog's face.

Dak knew Tog's sight would be superimposed with Dak's memory from his own point of view. He remembered the brown shape of Milah stalking past him as he lay in the Krusible, then his deep voice low in his ear. "Alright, so you've finally outgrown taunts of your heart breaking for that useless dame, Priya. It's nothing numerous hatchlings before you didn't figure out sooner. You haven't the control of mind or body needed to be among dragons, let alone any other species. Perhaps you should be sent to the deep, dark caverns of the Inner Mountain to die for all the good you are to anyone. Especially yourself. You're a worthless, mindless, idiotic, useless lump of scales. You don't deserve to even have wings, much less be allowed to use them, you pathetic troll. In this arena, you're mine and I promise you this; I don't care what it takes or how long, I will personally make sure you never...ever...leave the Rock Clouds, you mindless worm."

Tog blinked and Dak knew the memory in his mind had ended. He was back in his own body in Dak's cave. He stepped further into the cave then stumbled onto his backside, as if stunned for a moment. Suddenly he yelled, "That's it?! That's all it takes to make you imprison yourself in these rocks forever?!"

"That was just the last one, but it was worth it," Dak responded with a grin. "I told him his mother is an egg collector." Dak chortled at his joke as he curled up on the floor of the cave. It was the lowest of insults for a female and anyone related to her. Dak glanced up at his friend when he got no response.

One of Tog's eyes dilated in shock. Shaking his head slowly, Tog whispered, "You don't understand."

"What's to understand?" Dak's tail flicked in frustration. "It's Milah's fault! Those two have taunted us since we were hatchlings!"

Tog's horns seemed to elongate in his anger. "But at the Krusible, IT'S THEIR JOB, Dak!" Tog yelled again, striking the stone under him in his frustration.

Dak snaked his long neck away from his friend. "Why did Rakgar put them in charge of the Krusible, anyway?" he complained. "He only made it easier for them to rain havoc on their enemies."

A smooth voice answered from the entrance of the cave. "Milah and Mitashio passed the Krusible when they were only fifteen winters." Dak and Tog turned to see a small, bright green dragon with shining yellow eyes.

"Oh, wonderful!" Dak rolled his own midnight black eyes then rested his head on his claws. "Priya's here."

Priya had a short, rounded snout, and like most females, she didn't have a single horn on her head. She only had a few short spikes on the tip of her tail. Although her claws were shorter because of her stature, Dak knew from experience she didn't often miss her mark.

"Fifteen winters is the youngest any dragon has passed the Krusible," Priya continued as she slinked into the cave. "It was logical to put them in charge of testing when Thornac wished to be done." She dipped her head at Tog in greeting then shifted her narrowed gaze back to Dak. "I guess four claws does not a dragon make," she quoted the old saying, adding the negative. Before he left for the Krusible, Dak had insisted the ancient adage would hold true. He thought his fourth attempt would be the last. "Don't tell me they tried to make your heart break for me again, Dakoon," she sneered at him.

In his past attempts at the Krusible, the testers always had a tendency to tease Dak about his close friendship with Priya. In all these years, Dak's heart hadn't even come close to breaking for Priya, but that didn't prevent the insinuations that it would, thereafter pairing them as mates. Dak looked at Tog and jerked his head toward Priya. Tog put his nose in front of hers and gave her the same memory he had just received of Dak's last test.

After Priya blinked to clear her eyes, she waved the thought away with one claw. "They threaten the one thing you hold most dear, your freedom." She shook her head. "You have to admit they're very effective in their duties."

"But those two are worms!" Dak growled at her.

"Now, stop there, Dak!" Tog said firmly. "Although their wings are worthless, the surface worms are still actually dragons."

Dak waved a claw at the thought. "Yes, but they can't speak. They're not intelligent as real dragons, just like those two slugs in charge of the Krusible."

"They may not do it well, but Milah and Mitashio can speak," Tog countered.

Dak nodded. "You're right. The surface worms don't deserve such an insult, just because they aren't intelligent. Milah and Mitashio don't deserve to lick the slime from a worm's belly."

Tog nodded as well. "I'm sure worms everywhere would thank you – if they could."

"The brothers are only this hard on you," Priya insisted with a grin. "And you know why, Dakoon."

Tog snorted, "Dashing Dan." He chuckled quietly.

"Snap it, Tog," Dak scolded him.

Dashing Dan was a nickname Dak picked up as a hatchling. Dak was an entirely black dragon. Most dans, or male dragons, were shades of gray or brown, very dull and lusterless. However, they made up for their lack of color with their size. Dans were very large and usually had lots of horns, spikes and barbels. The dames, or female dragons, were usually covered with brilliant colors as well as patterns. Because Dak had only two horns on the sides of his head, which curved gracefully back like a gazelle's, and his scales were a deep lustrous black color, he appeared more feminine than most dans. However, dames usually found him very attractive. It was a good thing he was large too; he eventually fought his way away from the nickname.

Hearing the old nickname got under his scales and he took it out on Priya. "And don't call me Dakoon," he snarled at her.

"I've always called you Dakoon!" she stretched her neck to stare back at him. "Why should I change it now?"

Dak growled low, curling tighter on the ground. They'd had this conversation numerous times and Priya knew how Dak felt. He also didn't like his given name because it too closely resembled the prophecy of The One. Over thousands of winters the prophecy of The One, who would unite dragons and humans, had slipped from reverence to myth, from myth to story, from story to joke, and finally from joke to blasphemy. None of the dragons wanted anything to do with the idea that the dragons and humans would unite, so Dak hated any reference to the commonality.

"Yes," Tog piped up with mock sincerity, "she's always called us by our given names. She has no respect for chosen names."

Dak snorted at Priya in consent with his friend's words, but she answered without batting an eye. "On the contrary, I have the utmost respect for names." She cast her eyes down as her cat-like pupils dilated on a memory long buried from others.

"That's because there's nothing wrong with your name. It just means 'princess'," Dak said.

"And yours means 'dark one.' There's nothing wrong with that," she told him. "You should be proud of your name. And you," Priya jabbed her nose at Tog, "your name is Toggil because of the unique way your eyes move. You can see in two directions at once, an advantage any warrior might use majik to gain. Why would you try to overshadow it?"

"Tog means 'quick'," he retorted. "I'm a fast flier. I like it better."

"'Tog' and 'gil' mean 'quick' and 'eyes' in Faerie tongue."

Dak wrapped his claws over the spiny fans covering his ears. "Yes," he growled at her, "we know how fluent you are in Faerie tongue. It's a wonder you're not running around working majik with Visi instead of annoying us here."

"The faeries may claim their language is the most musical for majikal use," Tog added, "but I've heard majik can be done in any language. Do you use Faerie tongue in majik, Priya?"

She narrowed her eyes at him. "The faeries gave dragons the gift of speech. We use their language for names and titles out of respect for them. You know perfectly well I don't do majik. I've seen Visi do it, but I only know the language as a consequence of growing up with the witch dragon." Priya shrugged off the insult as she had many times, but Dak noticed she didn't say whether knowing Faerie tongue was a good or bad consequence.

Whenever this shadow came over her, Dak was reminded of the stark difference in their upbringing. Although the three friends had hatched about the same season twenty winters ago, no one knew of Priya's existence until seven winters later. While it was normal to wait a few moon cycles before introducing a hatchling, seven winters had been extraordinarily long. And to add to the mystery, the prophetess dragon, Visi, had raised her. No one other than Rakgar knew her real mother. To this end, his tongue had remained still in these long twenty winters. If he ever told Priya, she had also kept her silence. But when she was introduced after seven winters as the daughter of Rakgar, or Priya, she was readily accepted – if not for her status, for her beauty.

She snapped her maw at Tog then impaled Dak with her stare. "Perhaps we should call you Oon-Foslee, 'One Who Never Learns.' It seems you chose that name by your failure at the Krusible today."

He growled again as he eased his body from the floor. "My failure has nothing to do with any name except the ones Milah called me."

"It shouldn't matter what anyone calls you," she growled back. She kept her voice even, but she settled back on her haunches slightly as she mirrored his attack position. "Until you have respect for yourself, you won't pass the test."

"I will pass if I get a fair test!" He didn't wait for her response before he threw himself across the space between them.

Priya slipped to the side to avoid his jaws closing on her neck. "You'll never pass if you don't listen to the advice of your betters," she said calmly as she swiped him across the face and slashed him with her spiked tail. Dames may be small, but they're clever. That is what made them superior hunters.

The swat of her tail hurt, but Dak was used to it. "Like you?" he snarled at her as he feigned an attempt to snag her tail before he rolled to rake a claw across her face.

"Possibly," she said as she moved her face, but still received the claw lightly on her shoulder. "I passed my Krusible on the first attempt." She nipped at his leg before he could move it.

"I've been assigned!" Rather than watch his two friends tear each other apart – again – Tog blurted the surprise to interrupt.

Their frequent fights had never gone beyond anything they could heal by breathing fire on each other, but when Dak heard this, he stopped short. Priya bit him hard on the tail.

He cried out in pain, but Tog's words had cut deeper than Priya's action. He swung his head to face Tog. "You've been assigned?" he asked in shock.

"Of course he has," Priya answered for him, pushing Dak's leg from her belly.

Dak turned back to Priya. "To your contingent?"

"Where else?" she snapped, allowing her anger to show. "You knew I wanted you both. He passed his Krusible two winters ago. It's time Toggil stopped waiting for you to learn how to behave."

The cave rang with silence. Priya and Tog waited for Dak's response.

He finally shook his head slowly. "Why didn't you tell me?" he whispered to the floor. He knew he had seriously messed up. He might have been assigned too, had he passed the Krusible. He glanced up at Tog for an answer.

"They made me give my wyrd." He tried hard to avoid looking at Dak.

"Why?" he snarled in Priya's direction.

She stood up from her posturing crouch. "Dakoon, you have the distinction of being the first thing my father and I have agreed upon in tens of winters," she said. "We both agreed you should not be given any extra motivation to pass. You had to pass on your own convictions."

Dak nodded. He allowed his temper to simmer down before he spoke. "Well," he nodded again, "congratulations, Tog." Tog mumbled a small thanks. "Don't be so down," Dak tried to force himself not to sound upset. "It's not like you're leaving on a mission tomorrow."

"We are leaving on a mission tomorrow," Priya stated.

Dak's jaw fell open. "Tomorrow?"

"My father is sending me on an ambassadorship to the Desert Dragon Ruck," she said. "We leave tomorrow at sundown." The Desert Dragon Ruck lived in just that, the desert. Theirs was a small mountain range surrounded on every side by vast expanses of desert. Humans didn't dare traverse the blazing desert so the ruck lived in relative peace away from other creatures. They could easily keep watch over the surrounding desert and hunt freely in the forested mountains encompassing their desert. Because heat is so nourishing to a dragon, the desert is a desirable place. Priya's ambassadorship would be like an extended vacation – away from the cold winter in the Rock Clouds – with Tog and not Dak.

Dak closed his jaw and set his brain working. He began to pace in the small cave. "Perhaps," he said, "my father could speak with Rakgar."

"You can speak to him yourself," Priya told him.

Dak stopped to glare at her. "I don't understand."

"Of course you don't," she said. "Because you never take the time to."

"Is this your idea of a summons?" he asked, shaking his head.

"It's my father's idea of a kindly summons," she said. "He sent me instead of one of the official guard." Dak didn't move. He stood staring at her. "Or," she said, "you can ignore him. You've done that before. Fortunately for you, my father seems to have a spot in his heart for you."

"Him and all the huntresses," Tog mumbled again.

"Snap it, Tog," Dak said to him. "You can leave whenever you want."

"Are you kidding?" Tog gave a low grunt Dak knew was a chuckle. "I wouldn't miss this for all the sun in the desert."

2

Infliction

*R*akgar's lair, where Priya also lived, was the only one on the Inner Mountain besides Visi's. Visi lived near the top of the Inner Mountain, higher than the most determined dragons had the stamina to ascend. She used its isolation to keep from being plagued by every dragon in the ruck begging to know their future or asking for special majikal spells.

But Rakgar – which was Faerie tongue for "King" – lived with his daughter at the same altitude as the Rock Clouds, where the rest of the dragons lived. Although he was the dragons' ruler, he didn't think of himself as better than the rest. On the contrary, Rakgar (or Rakdar – as a female leader would be called) knew he was simply there to make decisions in the dragons' best interest. His role was to settle disputes between dragons and find their best assignments after they passed the Krusible. As dragons spent most of their time playing, laying around or occasionally eating, they weren't a difficult group to oversee.

Any dragon could challenge the Rakgar or Rakdar for their name and position. If they didn't want to give up their role, it meant a fight to the death or until one conceded. Priya's father, the current Rakgar, had gained his title more than twenty winters ago. Being the largest of all the dans, he had only been challenged twice since. Both times, after only a few scrapes from Rakgar's claws, the challenger withdrew.

As the three friends alighted on the lip of Rakgar's cave, Dak's nerves threatened to overtake him. He swung his head in Priya's direction. Without looking in her eyes, he asked, "Have you any indication of his feelings?"

She stayed silent until he met her eyes. "No."

Dak nodded once, rolled his shoulder, then entered. Priya and Tog followed, trying to keep to the shadows. Tog mumbled something about wanting to leave, but Dak knew his loyalty wouldn't allow him to be anywhere else. Terrified of what Rakgar might do or say, Dak would always be grateful for Tog's presence.

The narrow entrance to Rakgar's lair would only admit five or six dragons walking side-by-side, but the chamber beyond opened to reveal what many dragons believed to be the heart of the Inner Mountain. The foremost cavern was so large it could fit more than a hundred dragons, although the ruck didn't often need that capacity. In winter, dragons would often gather with their hatchlings or eggs to stay warm, but none had gathered yet.

Inside the cavern, thousands of wet spilling stone dripped from the ceilings with mound-like mates jutting up from the floor. Some of the dripping pairs met in the middle, forming columns scattered in the chambers, many as thick as a dragon's body. Two chambers separated by rock columns led off either side of the central chamber.

In one side chamber hung meat collected over the summer and autumn and dried by dragon fire. With winter just beginning, the chamber was packed with meat to the ceiling over two times the height of a dragon. When winter hunting grew scarce, many dragons had to be fed off the supply. If dragons went too long without eating, the fire in their own bellies would consume them, turning them to embers as swiftly as if someone had slit their throat in the night. As the leader of the ruck, Rakgar would be accused of murder if a hearty stock of dried meat wasn't available all winter.

Beyond the food chamber was a small chamber where Rakgar slept near the entrance so any dragon in the ruck could easily summon him.

Opposite the food supply, a small tunnel led away from the massive central chamber. Dak knew Priya's sleeping chamber was down the tunnel somewhere, but had never been down there. He had once come to find her to invite her to go to a lake with Tog and himself, but he met her a few steps into the tunnel. She was panting as if she'd flown from the other side of the mountain. Between gulps of air she unexpectedly raged that he would dare enter her chambers. That had been the oddest reaction he expected. Dragons were protective of their homes, but never to another dragon the way she had been to him. She apologized for her actions later that day while they explored the lake, but Dak never ventured near her lair again.

Very little light reached beyond the main chambers, with daylight coming only from the entrance and a large opening to the sky at the top of the central chamber. Occasionally dragons would explore beyond with the light from their own fire, but further caverns couldn't be used for much more than welcoming visiting dragons or the like. Most of the other tunnels off the main chamber were too small for any dragon to access.

The opening at the top of the chamber, big enough for two dragons to fly through if they tucked their wings slightly, showed a shock of light as the sun began to sink in the sky. Dak loped into the cavern to find his father, Tusten, sitting on the stone floor next to Rakgar. Behind them, the sun dazzled a small dragon-sized pile of gold, gems and other precious items.

Somehow, among the humans a rumor had grown. They believed dragons would spare their lives in a confrontation if they were given something shiny or sparkly. Dragons, however, didn't enjoy eating humans or any other intelligent creature; they thought it cannibalistic, so they encouraged the ruse with the humans. Many of the ruck deposited their "rewards" here since they had no other use for them. Some dragons thought human property made their lairs stink. This day, Dak could only smell the heated anger from the two dragons sitting in front of the pile of gold and gems.

"Shining days, Dromdan." "Dromdan" meant "father" in Faerie tongue. Dak greeted his father first out of respect. Even in Rakgar's presence, to do other-wise would be the utmost insult. "Shining days, Rakgar. You summoned me?"

"Today was your fourth attempt at the Krusible, was it not, Dakoon?" the enormous, pale gray dragon asked him. The numerous barbels hanging from his chin, cheeks and forehead gave him the look of a mas-sive gray lion. Short horns ringed his head and spikes ran down his back and spilled over his front shoul-ders. Along with his immense size, the overall effect made most dragons' scales shiver in fright. However, as Priya pointed out, Dak had always been a favorite with the king. Thus, Dak was probably the only beast besides his own father who was not intimidated in his presence. Until now.

"It was, Rakgar."

"And the sun still remains in the sky, does it not?" He lifted his head toward the dwindling ray of light from the ceiling, sending a ripple down the spikes along his back.

"It does, Rakgar."

"Considering your apparent inability to remain silent for an entire sun cycle, you must have quite a bit to say for yourself, Dakoon Ido Tusten." Rakgar cited his full name to remind Dak that his choices affected others. "Ido" meant "son" and put with his father's name it meant "son of Tusten". Tusten's name meant "trusted" because Tusten was Rakgar's most trusted advisor.

"I am as disappointed as anyone," Dak said.

"We are no longer disappointed, Ido." Tusten finally spoke up. The dark gray dragon rose from his seat by Rakgar to advance toward his wayward son. He was much like Dak in size and had the same long, pointed snout and two thick horns pointing off the back of his head. But Tusten also had smaller horns underneath those and spikes jutting from the backs of his front legs. These lifted slightly as he walked across the cold, rocky floor. In his anger, the spikes along his back and the scales on his neck and shoulders raised slightly as well. "The first time you failed, we were disappointed. 'He will certainly pass the second time,' we said." He nodded as he began to circle the black dragon.

"The second time you failed, we were surprised. 'How could he not pass?' we asked ourselves. 'Surely he is to be the greatest among us.'" He mocked surprise. "The third time you failed, we were confused. 'Perhaps something dreadful went wrong,' we said." He shook his head. "This time, Dakoon…" He stopped to glare into his son's eyes. "This time we are angry."

Dak sat in stony silence. "What's this?" His father bared his fangs. "Nothing to say?"

"I tried, Father," Dak finally answered.

"Tried?I TRIED?I" he growled with his teeth clenched and his top lip pulled back. "Have you learned nothing from the things I've taught you?"

"Perhaps he has too much of his mother in him?" Rakgar offered with a wry grin. "Niktiya was as impetuous a dame as ever lived; may her embers burn forever."

Niktiya, Dak's mother, had died five winters ago on a hunt. When a dragon died, their body instantly burned to a pile of smoldering embers. Dak remembered her as impatient, stubborn, proud and carefree as himself.

"No," Tusten shook his head again. "Niktiya's stubbornness helped her pass on her first try. This hatchling seems not to understand the importance of remaining silent. Maybe we should go over this again." He motioned with his claw to Priya and Tog hunkering in the corner. "You can even ask your friends for help if you don't know the answers."

"Father, I don't think this..." Dak began, but Tusten interrupted him.

"Dakoon," he raised his voice as if speaking to a hatchling. "Are we supposed to speak in front of humans?"

Dak sighed. "No, Father."

"Dakoon, describe humans?"

"They're monsters, Father. Unworthy of our acknowledgement or condescension."

"What do humans do to their young, Dakoon?"

"Beat them or eat them, whatever their fancy." The answers had been engraved on his tongue since his hatching.

"And what would humans do to us, if they knew of our intelligence?"

"Probably claw out our eyes to get to our brain. They're barbaric creatures, to be avoided at any cost." He intoned the words without feeling.

"Who may leave the Rock Clouds, Dakoon?" Tusten asked, carefully enunciating every word.

Dak remained silent.

"Who, my son?" His father repeated, baring his sharp teeth again.

Finally, Dak whispered, "Only those who prove their ability to remain silent in the Krusible."

Tusten turned back to Rakgar. "You see," he said, "he has been taught all these truths from the egg, and yet..." He looked back to Dak and shook his head. Dak's head sunk so low to the ground that he could smell several other dragons that had passed on the rock beneath.

"Has Toggil told you of his appointment?" Rakgar broke the silence.

"Just before we came here, Rakgar," Dak answered solemnly.

The silence in the cave rang louder than any roars his father could have made. Dak stood with his head drooping. Soon Rakgar spoke again. "Priya, Tog, Tusten, you will please go to the Krusible and ask another dragon to take over for Milah. Send him here to me."

The three acknowledged his request, and the two gray dragons and one small green dragon departed from Rakgar's lair. But Dak's sensitive hearing caught Priya's parting comment. "Perhaps we were a bit harsh."

To which his father replied, "No, indeed, young one. I fear we haven't been harsh enough."

Dak glared at the floor. In the silence, his mind wandered to his own embarrassing little secret. He had never told anyone except Tog for all these twenty winters. If his father or Priya found out, it would prove his ability to keep silent. But that would defeat the purpose, wouldn't it?

"You realize," Rakgar jolted him from his introspection, "that you were to be assigned to Priya's contingent should you pass the Krusible?"

"Yes, Rakgar." The three friends had been anticipating such an assignment for many winters.

"Your father will fly in your place."

"Yes, Rakgar."

Rakgar sighed. "What would you have me do, Dakoon?"

Dak thought a moment and then chanced a glance up at the powerful dragon. "I don't feel I can get a fair test here. Could you send me to the Desert Ruck to test at their next Krusible?"

Rakgar's face didn't twitch. He stared until Dak thought the leader might explode in anger at such an impertinent request. Eventually, he spoke. "A reasonable request under the circumstances." Dak waited a moment before he let himself breathe a sigh of relief. Perhaps, he might go with Priya and Tog after all. But then, why was he sending for Milah?

Rakgar stared down at Dak in silence. Dak couldn't find the bravery to look up at him, but instead watched the sunbeam creep across the floor. After what seemed like forever to Dak, an ugly brown dragon landed on the edge of Rakgar's cave.

"You sent for me, Rakgar?" Milah's sneering voice drifted across the cavern.

"Yes, Milah. Please join us."

Milah ignored Dak as he passed with his nose in the air, then turned back and sat down between Rakgar and Dak.

"Milah," Rakgar said, "please give me the memory of Dakoon's performance today."

Milah nodded then put his nose in front of Rakgar's. When he breathed into his face, the memory of only a short time ago returned to Dak's mind as well. Admittedly, his behavior seemed very infantile to him now.

Rakgar blinked as the memory cleared from his mind. He turned to look at Dak, who couldn't force himself to meet Rakgar's eyes. "Milah," he said softly, "accompanied by a fair number of other dragons, you came to visit me yesterday with a complaint about Dakoon."

"What?!" Dak's head whipped up.

But Milah answered the ruler. "Yes, Rakgar."

With eyes firmly fixed on Dak, Rakgar said, "Please inform Dakoon what that visit entailed."

Dak's eyes bounced between the two dragons in front of him, but narrowed at Milah as he turned to face him. "I, along with many of the ruck," he stated with a blank face, "feel that a dragon who cannot prove his worth within three attempts at the Krusible should not be allowed to test again nor ever allowed to go to the surface."

The fire in Dak's belly gave a nauseating gutter. What else had they been keeping from him? Might he never test again?

"Indeed," Milah's snide voice continued, "if a dragon cannot prove to the ruck his ability to keep his peace, then the essential secret of our intelligence would be at risk to the slightest whim of one so irresponsible. It is therefore imprudent to allow them to ever meet a human face-to-face."

"You're wrong," Dak growled into Milah's face.

Milah slid his lip back to bare his fangs in response.

"How so?" Rakgar asked instead.

Dak forced the snarl on his face to smooth away, then turned back to Rakgar. He breathed slowly to calm himself before he spoke. "Here," he answered, "there is no secret. When everyone around you knows you can speak, it seems a foolish task to hide it."

"You are the fool," Milah said through gritted teeth.

"But in front of a human," Dak ignored his comment as best he could, "it would be different. If your life hangs in the balance, there would be no choice but to keep your tongue still."

Milah raised an eyebrow. "Are you saying you want to test on the surface?"

"No" Dak acknowledged without looking at him. "But," he turned his most pleadful eyes to Rakgar, "If I could test under different circumstances. In a different venue, perhaps?"

Rakgar hummed then nodded. "Yes."

"What?!" This time it was Milah's turn to be incensed.

"I will allow you to go to the Desert Ruck to test."

Both Milah and Dak stood with their mouths gaping at their leader. Milah recovered his senses first. "There would be a mass outcry for such leniency!" he roared. "I demand some form of punishment for his continued failure!"

"And there will be," Rakgar said. Dak's smile faded before it could begin. "The Krusible is held at the opening of each new season. Dakoon, you will not travel with Priya and the contingent at this time, but must wait fifteen moons until you will be allowed to test again. You must also use the time given to practice your silence with Milah and Mitashio every day." Dak's jaw fell open as he felt the fire in his belly – and thus, his life – all but stomped out.

Fifteen moons. One year. Five seasons. Time held great meaning for him at this moment. No dragon had ever been forced to wait so long to test again. And practicing silence with the brothers would be paramount to torture. "At that time, you will be allowed to travel to the desert with Milah and Mitashio and undertake the Krusible there," Rakgar finished.

Milah's jaw closed in a smug grin. "Most wise, Rakgar."

Still in shock, Dak almost didn't notice Rakgar walk over to him. "I'm sorry, Dakoon. But I hope this will be for your good."

"As do I," Dak choked. "Am I dismissed?" He'd had enough humiliation for the day. When Rakgar answered in the affirmative, Dak turned to limp toward the exit.

"Dakoon," Rakgar called him again.

What else can he do to punish me? Dak asked himself. He turned his head to the side to show Rakgar he was listening, but didn't meet his eyes.

"Know this," Rakgar's deep tones reached him. "If you fail again, you will be given no more attempts."

3

Shaman Warning

Young Prince Philip sat in the far right of three thrones in an alcove farthest away from the double doors into the audience hall. On the wall behind, three large portraits hovered over him: his father, King Paudie; his mother, Queen Linea; and a replica of his own youthful countenance. Tapestries of former kings and lesser gods enshrouded the other throne room walls. Blue bunting trimmed in silver drooped over the thrones. Philip was grateful this room didn't have a fireplace; instead, large glass domes fixed to the walls at intervals majikally magnified any natural light. He stared straight ahead, trying to ignore the bead of sweat trickling down the back of his neck.

Philip had attended audiences in Kingstor castle in training with his father, so he'd insisted on being dressed in the lightest summer materials his extensive wardrobe had to offer. But even wearing light cotton breeches and a silken gray tunic, his undergarments still soaked his skin. He wished so many people didn't attend these occasions.

Dozens of courtiers lingered in the audience hall, hoping to be the first with any interesting news. Women dressed in dazzling shades of silk with their hair piled on their heads in tight curls watched the prince with blushing eyes. Men thrice his age wore their titles and honors on their cloaks and watched him with more scrutiny. The overall effect of the cloaks, dresses and people made the hall downright stifling despite the gentle snowfall outside the immovable stained glass windows.

The nobles in attendance had been waiting for something to happen of late. Only a few months ago Philip's father, King Paudie had taken seriously ill, leaving the middle and most ornate of the thrones bare. Philip was only sixteen. He had been raised to rule and schooled in politics almost since his birth, so Royal General Bragon, the man who commanded the king's troops within the castle, had insisted the prince step forward or risk a coup. When Philip relieved the Lord Traggit (one of the local nobles), who had stepped in for his father in time of need, he realized the man acquiesced only reluctantly.

But today, he met with the nobles. A tedious task in itself, but necessary. Many of them squabbled over ownership of spits of land or taxes on goods. He had no patience for the rich men of his land trying to get richer through their greed.

"The village on the west side of the river has always paid taxes to my house, My Liege," Lord Harcast was saying. Two tall feathers sticking up from the back of his poufy hat must be meant to give him the appearance of a dragon, but in combination with his huge front teeth and turned-up nose, instead gave the idea of a rabbit. "Lord Surcund can't insist they start paying him taxes as well!"

"They have always paid taxes to me," Lord Surcund insisted. Surcund was a short, fat fellow with a thin mustache over his lip and almost no hair on his head. The golden buttons on his overcoat stretched so tightly over his barrel chest that Philip sat in fear they would explode any moment. "It is you who forces them to pay more than their due."

"That's a lie!" Harcast yelled.

"Your claim is a lie!" Surcund yelled back. Philip thought his buttons gave an audible creak.

As the two lords continued bickering, Prince Philip leaned over to General Bragon who stood at his right-hand side. Although Bragon made no movement towards him, Philip knew his general would hear every word he said. "Send a man secretly to this village," he whispered to his advisor. "Have him bring me a long-time villager to give me the truth of it. I'll never get it from these two frauds."

General Bragon gave the slightest bow of his head, then slipped out of the court through a side door.

"Gentlemen!" Philip announced loudly as he stood, cutting off their argument. The two nobles stopped to stare at the young prince. Although a fraction of their age, Philip's disposition demanded obeisance from everyone he met. If not for his title, then certainly for his stature. Even without the dais, he stood inches over a tall man. "Tomorrow is my sixteenth birthday. I have many preparations to make and don't want any ill feelings at my celebration. Won't you both please stay at the castle until the feast? Then we can settle this matter after." The village was easily a day's journey away on horseback, and another day to return with an impartial villager, but the arrangement would have to do for now.

"Happy to do it, Sire."

"Many congratulations to you, Sire."

The pompous roosters bowed themselves out of the audience chamber, leaving Philip to heave a sigh. These were the same types of nobles General Bragon had warned him against. They would support the other nobles in the room that watched Philip's every move carefully, if ever they decided to try to unseat the prince. He had no intention of playing favorites with either of them – and therefore arousing the suspicion of the other nobles – but knew he had to rule with a firm hand to keep them in line. He turned to his personal servant, Murthur to whisper, "Put them off for a couple of days, I need to – " His words cut off as the great double doors into the audience chamber pushed open.

"Sire!" A guard knelt on one knee in front of Philip. One hand held the hilt of his sword, while the other saluted at his chest in a tight fist, thumb in, small finger out as if stabbing himself. "Two faeries have arrived. They insist on seeing you at once."

General Bragon entered soon enough to hear the guard's message. He and Philip shared a glance. "See them in," Philip answered.

The guard stood and bowed at the waist. As he left through the double doors, General Bragon leaned in closer to the Prince. "A visit from the faeries?" he mused. "It must be important. They don't visit often."

"Important, yes," Philip answered. "But I don't trust faeries."

"Why not, Sire?"

"I'm not sure. I guess I don't trust anyone whose face I can't search at my leisure."

The double doors opened again to reveal two heavily cloaked figures. Black cloth covered the bottom half of the deep cowls in their thick, brown traveling cloaks, as if to only allow a black hollow for anyone else to see. Dark gloves covered their hands seemingly all the way up their arms and leather bindings hid their feet and legs where they protruded from their cloaks. Their transparent wings were uncovered and folded neatly against their backs as they glided into the audience chamber. Unless you looked closely, you might think them only a design of the cloth. One of them carried a small bag over his shoulder. Other than the bag, they displayed no difference between the two of them.

"Prince Philip of the Noble Kingdom of the Five Swords of Avonoa," the faerie without the bag addressed him. "Allow me to introduce myself." Bowing at the waist, he waved one hand in front of him. "I am Sha Kradik, from the Faerie realm of Reteig. This is my apprentice, Ortym." The faerie with the bag also bowed.

"Sha?" Philip asked. He had been educated in Faerie culture, but had rare occasion to experience it first-hand. Although the faeries were friendly with humans, unlike the ferocious centaurs, they kept to themselves. "You're majishuns?"

"Much more than majishuns," Kradik answered with another smaller bow. "Even my apprentice is a practiced Shaman. We have come with a grave warning for Your Majesty, and to offer our assistance."

"A warning?" Philip asked, although his thoughts lingered over how he would be able to tell these identical creatures apart when Ortym put the bag down.

"Our branch of expertise is in dragons. We study them, My Lord, and have seen in them recent behaviors to bode ill for the Noble Kingdom."

"What behaviors?"

Kradik gestured to Ortym so he stepped closer to the prince. "Amidst my future reading, I have seen six male and one female dragon leave the Rock Clouds," he said in a nasal voice – giving Philip the answer to his own dilemma. "As you might or might not be aware, dans – that would be the males – carry a single egg each and they need only one female to fertilize all of them."

"What would this behavior mean to us?" Philip asked.

Kradik answered. "They mean to expand their domain, Prince."

"But the Rock Clouds are nearer the Courageous Kingdom," Philip responded. "Why do you not advise King Torodov of this danger?"

"We have looked into the futures of the dragons and King Torodov's, as well as your own, Prince," Ortym answered him. "The dragons mean to inhabit the very mountains overlooking your castle."

Philip's brow creased with concern as the nobles and courtiers in the hall began to murmur. Dragons living so close to humans would mean the people of his kingdom would be in danger every moment of their lives. Not to mention the damage dragons could do to their flocks and livelihoods. "But," Philip couldn't believe it. "They've never lived so near humans, or any other creatures, for that matter. Why would their habits change now?"

"Who's to say, My Lord?" Ortym answered. Philip began to wonder if Ortym was the dragon specialist. "They're creatures of instinct. Perhaps the hunting is better here. Perhaps the Rock Clouds are overwhelmed with dragons. Whatever the reason, if it is permitted to happen, your kingdom will be in grave danger."

"And not just your kingdom, Majesty," Kradik continued. "Their hunting grounds will grow to encompass much more of Avonoa than just the Noble Kingdom."

Philip hung his head in thought for a moment. He couldn't allow dragons to roost so near his own stronghold. But what could be done about it? He looked up at the two faeries. "Did you say you've come to offer assistance?"

"Yes, My Lord," Kradik answered.

"What course of action would you propose?" he asked them.

"An ambush, My Lord."

"We can tell you where they will emerge from the Torthoth Mountains," Ortym said.

"We have the majikal powers to eradicate them," Kradik said, while gesturing to Ortym again.

Philip's natural suspicion, cultivated in him from childhood, crept up again. "Why would you do this?" he asked, struggling to attain eye contact with the two mysterious beings. "Faeries have always tried to protect the dragons," or so he had been taught. "Why are you now willing to assist in their destruction?"

The two faeries turned to each other and Philip wondered if they could see each other through the shrouds. Ortym nodded.

"We have looked into every detail of your future," Kradik said. "If the Noble Kingdom falls to the dragons, the Noble Sword of Avonoa will be lost. With only four swords left, the kingdoms will divide, and a civil war will bring about the downfall of Avonoa.

After a century of fighting, dragons will overrun the last human survivors, and humans will cease to exist in Avonoa."

Philip couldn't contain his bewilderment. His mouth hung open in the same undignified manner his father had chastised him for displaying in his youth. Even the nobles present gave a collective murmur.

The Noble Sword lost? Many millennia ago, the faeries had made a gift of five swords with majikal powers to the humans. Each kingdom retained a sword to ensure the balance of power. In the event of a disagreement among kingdoms, the other sovereigns were sought to define the proper cooperation and resolve the matter. In this way, the five kingdoms (or four kingdoms and one queendom) had enjoyed stable peace for many thousands of years. The loss of a sword would bring chaos to Avonoa.

Thousands of villages and cities spread across the Kingdoms of the Five Swords of Avonoa. Millions of human lives depended on Philip's decision. But he really had no choice.

He closed his mouth and searched the floor for words. "You claim you can help us avoid this devastation?"

"Absolutely, Sire," Ortym said.

Kradik stepped forward. "We will accompany the men ourselves."

"Very well." Philip straightened himself on the throne. "General Bragon," he turned to his advisor. "You'll gather twenty men to go – "

"Twenty men will not be enough against seven dragons," Kradik interrupted. "Especially with a female among them."

"Fine," Philip scowled at the dark recess of his cowl. He didn't take kindly to being interrupted or corrected in front of his own people. "Thirty, but not a single man more." He might have been willing to send more men, but he had to assert his will over the foreigners.

Kradik nodded. Philip waved to his personal servant. "Murthur will show you to your rooms in the castle. We'll discuss the details of your plan at dinner tonight."

"Thank you, Your Majesty," both faeries bowed, "but we prefer to keep our accommodations closer to nature than the castle affords. We have rooms in the village outside of Kingstor."

"A little far away, don't you think?" Philip said. "What if I need your assistance?"

"Don't worry, Sire," Ortym spoke up. "We will know when you need us."

"Until tonight," Kradik said before the two faeries bowed again and left the audience hall.

"Bragon," Philip's eyes bored unblinking into the double doors as they closed behind his guests. "Why do I feel as if I've just struck a bargain with a devil?"

Bragon's response wasn't encouraging. "Two devils, Sire."

4

Nervous Escape

Six pairs of dragon eyes stared unblinking at Dak. Priya was the first to nod.

"My father's rulings are usually firm," she told Dak. "I don't see why you would expect otherwise."

"But this has gone too far," Tog said, as Dak ambled away from them to sink next to the wall of the cave. "Rakgar didn't even punish us when we stole food our fifth winter. And he knows Milah and Mitashio are the problem."

"Exactly why Dak needs to overcome their antagonism so he may progress in the world" Tusten interjected.

Priya nodded again. "If Dak can learn to ignore Milah and Mitashio, no matter what cruelty they impose, humans should be easy."

"But for so long?" Tog questioned.

"Dak should be grateful he gets another chance at all," Priya retorted. Dak's low growl rumbled through the cave.

"Enough," Tusten said. "I see the hunt returning. Let's stoke our fires so we may fight later." He slipped out the entrance into the darkening sky. Priya narrowed her eyes at Dak then dashed to follow.

"Come on, Dak," Tog coaxed his friend. "You have to eat. Not many others will know what happened yet. And it might be a while before a big kill like this comes in again."

Dak rose slowly, but eventually left with his friend to join a large portion of the ruck at the feeding grounds.

Dragon dames aspired to be one thing in their lives, mighty huntresses. Females were the providers. Especially in the Rock Clouds, huntresses provided food for the entire ruck. A dragon could go weeks without eating, but females had to hunt almost every day. Small animals like rabbits, squirrels and foxes lived in the floating mountains, but they were mostly used as practice for the hatchlings.

Sometimes the dames hunted in large groups in order to bring back larger game like paquars. A paquar had large, bony protrusions on the head, but its body was strong, with lots of meat below the neck, especially in its muscular legs. Paquars were larger than even

Rakgar and so provided sustenance to many dragons. Other times, dames hunted in small packs or on their own and brought back small animals like deer or pigs. These were often better food for the hatchlings or fledglings because they were easier to tear into with their smaller claws and teeth.

Occasionally a dan might get it into his head to go hunting as well. It didn't happen often, as the dans were responsible for training hatchlings and protecting the Rock Cloud home. But if they had nothing more important to do or no little one to care for, they were welcome to try, as long as they had passed the Krusible. It was well known that dans were not nearly as quiet or nimble as dames and therefore made clumsy hunters.

As it was the start of winter, the larger kills would soon become scarce. Many dragons already had a hardy supply of meat hanging in their caves which they had slowly dried with their own fires. This would serve to feed them over the next three moons. The cold winter days would force the dragons to eat more often than they did in warm seasons. But while there was fresh meat, as many as could would take advantage of it.

As the three friends flew to the feeding grounds near the Krusible on the Inner Mountain, many others joined them. Dak marveled at the variety of dragons in the ruck. Although the males were all gray or brown, color variations made it easy to tell the dans apart, as well as the number and size of horns and spikes. Some had transparent wings like a dragonfly and could hover in mid-air. Some, like Prakyndar, a dragon a few winters younger than Dak, had smaller wings making it necessary to beat them twice as fast as the dragons with larger wings to fly the same distance. A few dragons in the ruck had only two rear claws. This trait hailed mostly from the Island Ruck, who got along by using a long sharp hook claw at the wing joint.

Dak had heard that many Island Ruck dragons also had webbed claws to help them swim. Swim! Dak always wondered what dragon in their right mind would immerse themselves in water. As younglings Dak and Tog once dared each other to submerge themselves in a lake. Neither of them had the nerve, although Dak had dunked his whole head under the surface. The Island Ruck claimed they swam to hunt large water creatures. But they lived on their own large island so far on the other side of Avonoa that not many in the Rock Cloud Ruck saw them very often. Dak and Tog had sworn to each other that when they could leave the Rock Clouds, they would go to the Island Ruck and see if they really did swim.

The environment in which each ruck lived produced many strange characteristics among dragons. For instance, Dak once met a dame from the Northern Ice Ruck who had narrow green scales almost like the quills on a porcupine. When he asked her about them, she said they sealed together to protect her from the cold. But she said her scales weren't as developed as others. She claimed her Rakdar had full-grown feathers instead of scales!

The Rock Cloud Ruck females had nice normal scales, like those on a snake which fit together and covered well, working along four useful legs. Some of the dames, in shades of blue or green, had bifurcated tails or tongues. He had seen one yellowish-green dame with only one eye in the middle of her forehead, and it was said she could see things other dragons could not. Another had webbed claws as well as webbing under her forelegs. She won every flying race known to the dragons.

The Desert Ruck dames flaunted bright colors of red and orange. Dak had seen many of them over his lifetime. Their thin scales could soak up the heat of the sun which burned year-round in the desert. Most of them were lean because they didn't need to eat as often as other rucks. The sun provided plenty of heat for them to be comfortable without food for long intervals. Whenever a dragon came from the desert, they constantly complained about the chill in the air, even in the summer. After living in the Rock Clouds for a while, they would shed their thin scales to grow larger thicker scales protecting them from the cooler temperatures. The complaints would ease, but most of them would often reminisce about the comfort of the desert. One of these desert dames was the dark red, Surneen.

Surneen was blood red with large orange spots all over her, from head to tail. Her wing membranes were orange as well and her eyes were blood red. As Tog and Dak arrived at the feeding grounds ahead of most of the others, they dug into the shoulder of a small lydik

Surneen had brought back from her hunt. Although normally a coarse, hairy animal, somewhat like a boar with antlers and claws, the outside of the lydik had been burned to a perfect crispy black while leaving the inside soft and dripping. Tog always thought Surneen toasted her kills exactly right. She didn't, but Dak knew Tog had a spot in his heart for Surneen.

Once, out of impertinence, Dak asked Surneen how she could possibly stay hidden from her prey in a forest. She grinned her fangs at him. "With either the sunrise or the sunset at my back, I can hide in plain sight." She explained some of the hunting and camouflage techniques dames were taught, and shared how she usually sat at the top of the hill at sunset and waited for prey to come to her. Tog couldn't take his eyes off of her as she spoke, but also couldn't say a word. Dak noticed how she pointedly refused to look at him as well.

Tog had been right that word about Dak's predicament had not spread. The other dragons at the feeding ground didn't give him a second glance. However, he hadn't filled his stomach even halfway when he heard a hum behind him. His heart dropped as he recognized the stench of the two muddy brown dragons he had left in the Krusible while the sun shone.

"Well, Dakoon," Milah hissed as he circled his foe. "Sounds like we'll be spending plenty of time getting to know each other in the next fifteen moons."

"Good thing we already know all about you." Mitashio murmured. "Makes our task easier." He grinned.

"But yours," Milah sneered at Dak, "will not be so easy." The pair laughed at their wit.

"Go freeze yourself," Dak mumbled the curse at them.

"Just keep eating," Tog whispered to him. "They'll go away."

"Yes," Mitashio said. "Enjoy your freedom while you can."

"Make sure you eat plenty," Milah added. "You'll need the extra fire."

Dak ground his claws into the rock underneath to keep himself from attacking – his partially eaten lydik now forgotten.

"Fifteen moons of extra training," Milah said loudly so some of the dragons looked their way. "Sounds like Rakgar thinks you've learned nothing more than a hatchling already knows."

Dak could take the degradation no longer. He spun on the two dragons as they chuckled at his predicament. He growled and they growled back. With bloody fangs bared, Dak answered clearly, "I promise the two of you this, for the next fifteen moons I will not say another word to either of you." With a belch of flame, he tore into the sky away from the feeding grounds.

—

Avonoa's three moons hung overhead throwing their borrowed light on Dak. Sitting atop the single jutting rock, he knew himself to be nearly invisible to other dragons. His body would be dappled with light as the starry sky wrapped around him.

"Knew you'd be here." Tog's voice came from beneath him as he climbed up to his friend.

From this protrusion they had scrutinized the surface world beneath them as the gods do. They could see dragons flying to or from the Rock Clouds. As hatchlings their fathers taught them to fly from here because the rock hung perilously at the top of a short cliff towards the bottom of their mountain. Their families both had homes further above in this sailing mountain.

What the pair liked most about this rock was that, by all known laws of the world, the rock shouldn't stay in its current position, let alone hold the weight of two fully grown dragons. The rock looked as if it might fall at any moment, but had remained steadfast through all these winters. The two young friends enjoyed the thrill of anticipating someday seeing the rock tumble to the bottom of the mountain below.

All of the other dragons in the ruck, including Dak's own parents, assumed the two best friends sat up here almost every night of their lives enjoying the view at nighttime. But Tog was the only dragon alive to know of Dak's most embarrassing secret – the same secret that would prove to his father and everyone else his ability to withhold from others. It was common belief among dragons that the darker a dragon's scales, the better they could see in the dark. But as far as he knew, Dak was the only exception to this rule. He confided in Tog when they were both very young and ever since, the two sat atop this rock to practice his night vision. However, as much as the two tried, they could not improve Dak's eyes. The best they could do was improve his other senses in order to compensate.

Tog took up watch next to his best friend, and mirroring Dak's pose, he wrapped his tail around himself for added warmth. Both alert, but introspective. Soon the memory of the worst day of Dak's life would spread through the entire ruck like a disease. He knew it had already started.

"I'm sorry, Dak," his friend offered after a time.

"It's not your fault," Dak answered. "You were bound by your wyrd." When a dragon gave his wyrd, it was more serious than an oath or a promise. If he broke his wyrd, the dragon to which he gave it would then own his life; that is, if a dragon broke his wyrd, the recipient could choose to either kill him or forgive him. He turned to his lifelong friend of twenty winters. "You have always been as good as your wyrd."

Tog hung his head in shame. "Who knows," he shrugged. "Maybe the extra training will do some good. You could get some good fodder on those two brown worms."

Dak couldn't trust himself to answer.

After a moment, Tog chuckled softly. "Do you remember when we were hatchlings and you found a leppi floating by your cave?"

Dak grinned at the memory despite his best efforts. "You were terrified of it."

"Well," Tog cocked his head looking at the leppi in his mind's eye. "A big, round body drifting through the heavens with nothing but a single tentacle to propel it? It seemed unnatural to me."

"As I recall, you ran and told my father."

"In vain," Tog shook his head. "You pawed at it while we begged you to stop!"

Dak chuckled. "I suffered for it too, didn't I?"

"I thought you'd been struck by lightning when it shocked you."

"I couldn't see for three days!" Dak roared.

When their laughter died away, Tog sighed, "You should've listened." Then he tacitly crawled away.

Once his friend was out of sight, Dak took a long deep breath of the frozen night air. When he was sure he was alone again, he slipped silently behind the massive stone.

———

The following day, everyone left Dak alone. Milah and Mitashio went to Rakgar to complain of their pupil not showing for his lessons. But Rakgar's mercy once again kindled for Dakoon. He insisted Dakoon need not start his training with the brothers until after Priya and her contingent departed for the Desert Ruck. Tusten came to tell his son this, but found him fast asleep in their lair. He assumed Dakoon had been up most of the night brooding, and couldn't bring himself to wake him. But as soon as Tusten left, Dak opened his eyes and again slipped out of the cave.

When the sun waned in the sky, Tog found Dak sitting upon their rocky lookout again.

"I've come to say good-bye," he announced from behind.

"Shining days, freeg," Dak said without turning, using the affectionate term for "friend".

"Clear skies to you," Tog responded to the back of his best friend's head. The gray dragon turned with resignation to leave, but stopped and turned back. "Dak," he said low. He knew he could hear him. "Please," he paused to search for words, "don't be impulsive. Stay focused, and we'll fly from this place together next time." He waited for an answer.

Dak hesitated to speak his mind, but when Tog started to turn away again, he loosed his tongue before he didn't have another chance. "Tog," he said without turning to his friend. "Do you think...I mean...If our parents hadn't already been friends..." he wasn't sure how to voice his concerns. "Milah and Mitashio always follow the rules ... and you always follow the rules... and you always get upset when I don't and...." he let his voice disappear in an unasked question.

"No one else chooses our path or our friends, Dak," Tog whispered.

After a minute of silence, Dak said, "Clear skies to you, my friend." With a sigh, Tog crawled away.

Once again, when he disappeared, Dak scrambled behind the rock. He clawed at the bottom of the rock, scraping it with his sharp claws. He didn't even know if his plan would work; some of the rocks from these mountains floated and some didn't. Some fell to the earth only to rise later, or would float from the instant they fell. Some rocks tumbled to the Inner Mountain to remain forever. He vaguely noticed the sun dip behind the trees. When he felt the air get colder, he realized the sun had set and he crawled back onto the top of the projection.

He arrived in time to see the formation fly out from behind a nearby mountain, one small green dragon in the middle of six larger ones. Three brown dragons led the triangle formation, with two gray on either side of Priya and one gray in back. Dak's frustration built up inside him. He roared at the top of his lungs, loosing a blazing stream of fire in his anger. It was now or never. Priya and her contingent flew down the mountain toward the trees below. If Dak took much longer in his quest, he might lose them.

Dak scratched at the bottom of the rock with every bit of strength in his claws. His mountain and this boulder were pointing too far south, making the start of his chase longer than ideal, but it was his only hope of escape. He consoled himself thinking that darkness would cover him. He wedged himself between the clinging rock and the mountain behind it, and pushed. He could see Tog in the distance, almost to the twisted tree. Miraculously, the rock jolted.

"Come on," he pleaded with his stubborn foe. He leaned his shoulder into it, but it refused to move any more. In the back of his mind he could see why they had never seen this stubborn lump move. "Come on," he begged as his quarry passed the funny tree and gained on the horizon. Even if he liberated this rock and himself, he would begin his chase far behind.

He scuttled to the opposite side of the rock, hoping to pull it free. As he clung to the front face of the rock four claws landed brutally on top. Although relieved to feel it jostled more, Dak looked up to see who had caught him in his escape.

His eyes rose from the four white claws to the drooping wings and tattered, graying white scales of Visi. She was rarely seen and even more rarely heard. Many assumed the old dragon, who had lived longer than any dragon in all existence, had lost her mind attempting to read too many futures. Yet many still attempted the ascent to the top of the Inner Mountain to appeal to her when the need was great.

"This," she said as if she had a fireball stuck in her throat, "is for what you'll call me at the bottom." With that, she muttered a few incoherent words, then wedged herself behind the rock.

Dak had dug his talons into the rock while trying to pull it free. As Visi spoke he stared at her in stunned silence. Once she disappeared behind the rock, he blinked, wondering what she meant and what he should do next. But before he had a moment to think, with a grating sound, the rock lurched backwards on top of Dak. For a moment, instinct tried to force him out of the way, but he closed his eyes and forced himself to dig in even tighter.

When a dragon lifts himself into the air, his stomach never churns because he is in control. When a hatchling flies for the first time, they might occasionally experience the rolling of the innards as flight is achieved. But as Dak fell backwards, pressed against the rock with his wings tucked firmly against his body, the fire in his belly gave a sudden shudder as wind washing over a flame.

The rock came free of its thousand-year home to tumble without restraint through the sky. Normally, The Watch dragons who guarded the edges of the Rock Clouds would investigate such a disruption. But behind him through the clouds, Dak heard Visi's voice call out to whomever might listen. "Oops! My tail slipped!" She cackled her hideous laughter and disappeared into the night.

As Dak fell through the sky, all he could do was pray to the gods that The Watch didn't see him attached. If Rakgar caught him attempting this, he would surely be killed, seeing as he couldn't be banished. But his mind clung as tightly to Visi's words as his claws clung to the rock. She had said, "...at the bottom."

Fortunately for Dak, none of The Watch noticed him attached to the debris. Unfortunately for Dak, the stone hit the barren land at the bottom of the Inner Mountain hard. Had it been summer season, he might have been able to jump from the rock to slip into the forest, but as even the smallest of shrubs were stripped of leaves, he would be forced to wait for the rock to roll further among taller leafless growth.

His impervious scales protected him from too much injury, but while the stone rolled and bounced he felt as if Visi had decided to use him for battering practice. Whether the crazy dame was helping him or not, Dak felt like two giants were kicking him between them as he rolled with the stone. He remembered the time Milah and Mitashio challenged Dak and Tog to a contest of lifting rocks. Unknown to the two friends, their rivals had hollowed out large boulders with their fire, giving them a distinct advantage. Dak ended up getting smashed by a boulder almost as large as he was before Tog discovered the deception.

As he debated whether he should have stayed in the Rock Clouds to take the same abuse from Milah and Mitashio, his stone assassin rolled to a stop amidst the barren tree trunks. Dak's claws broke away and he fell onto his back with a soft thud. "That mother hen pecker," Dak whispered the worst curse for a dame he could think of then came to rest under the naked thatched branches.

He caught his breath, listening for any sentries that might come to investigate. Nothing moved in the still forest around him. Dak chanced to pick his head off the frozen, packed dirt under him. Less looking, but more listening he scanned around him. Nothing. He rolled onto his stomach to get his bearings. He knew Priya and her group had flown in the direction of the desert.

Dak hadn't thought about how he would follow them. Taking off among the trees was extremely difficult, not to mention dangerous to the fragile wing membranes. Plus, he couldn't launch himself into the sky at this point without being seen by The Watch. Whether he came from the air or the forest below, if a sentry saw him follow the group, they would intercept him. So he took off at a gallop in the direction of the desert.

5

On The Hunt

Dak ran unsparing. His fire burned hot inside him, but as he ran he noticed the difference of frozen earth and rock under his claws. Occasionally he came to a clearing, but he judged his proximity too close to the Inner Mountain to risk flight. He knew he would be forced to fly or lose his pursuit, but couldn't risk it too soon, so as not to be caught. He dashed around the edges of the clearing, making sure no one from the Rock Clouds would notice the movement in the night. But no matter how pitilessly he pressed himself, the Inner Mountain seemed to follow him in his escape. Eventually, he worried he might lose Priya's group, so when he came to another opening in the trees, he decided to risk it.

An etching in the ground left proof of a small creek having once run through the clearing, with two big rocks on either side of it. Dak jumped with all fours onto the closest rock. Even though his legs trembled from the run, he bunched his muscles then flung himself into the sky above the branches. In order to clear the treetops he fought against a stale winter breeze pulling him down. But warmth immediately spread into his relieved limbs as he gained flight. He pumped his wings to lift higher into the cold night air. Hovering long enough to look back at the Rock Clouds, he realized he'd run farther than he thought.

He got his bearings of the landscape around him. From his old rock perch at home, he often saw the forest he had just run through. He could also see the ribbon of river cutting through the land of the centaurs. The dragons called it Centaur River. That is where he could go for safe haven if need be, since the centaurs were friends to the dragons – and no other creatures, including humans. But beyond this point, the land had been a hazy blur to Dak until now.

A mountain range spread in front of him on the horizon. He could see a little of the ebb and flow of the land in front of it, but his vision again blurred with the darkness. He knew the desert dragons were surrounded by mountains; therefore, he assumed they must be on the other side. But the flight there had to be a good two-day journey as the dragon flies. He flew off as fast as his wings could carry him.

While he soared, he planned his next steps. Foremost, he must find the contingent. Then he must follow at a distance. He had been running for what seemed like a lifetlme. Although a dragon can run as fast as they can fly when they're unhindered, Dak was sure the frozen forest had slowed him considerably.

Next, he debated whether he should reveal his pursuit to Tog – if he ever found them – but decided against it unless absolutely necessary. While Tog was fiercely loyal, he was also honest. If any of the other dragons asked him if they were being followed, he would tell the truth.

His final goal would come once they reached their destination. He must throw himself on the mercy of the Desert Rakdar. Dak hoped against hope that she might see fit to let him live. If not, Dak must fight to escape the Desert Ruck and head for safety with the centaurs.

The moons had risen to almost the apex of the sky when Dak had taken flight. The sky sparkled with stars above him. Occasionally he thought he could see the group of dragons he pursued, but his eyes weren't trustworthy. With his wings fighting against the cold wind, he wouldn't be able to hear anything either. The moons eventually began to cross over him.

Dak struggled to keep his wings pumping as the moons descended in the sky. He had been awake all day preparing his escape and he had never flown for this long before. His eyelids kept sagging, but some-how he kept them up. He listened to his heart beating and felt the crisp air rushing through his lungs. The forest below him remained eerily silent and as unforgiving as the sky above.

Dak had never been down to the surface before. He'd never known the blistering cold of the winters below. With no clouds overhead, the surface temperature dropped dangerously low for a dragon. In the Rock Clouds winter was only just tolerable, but as he flew now over the brittle forest he realized just how dangerous his choice might turn out to be.

The five seasons of the year in Avonoa – Fall, Spring, Summer, Autumn and Winter – had three moon cycles each. Dragons thrived on heat; it was the essence of their being. Without heat and fire, they die. Therefore, winter was the most difficult for dragons, with snow and cold and ice endangering their internal fire. Some dragons tried to sleep the winter away, but their attempts were usually in vain. Only the ice dragons could withstand such treatment.

Following winter came fall. Fall was also treacherous for dragons' fire because rain fell ruthlessly and although not as cold as winter, the storms of fall could be dangerous for flight. Especially if one attempted to fly through thunderclouds.

However, the snow melted off from the rains of fall and spring brought forth new plants. Then came the welcome respite of summer. Summer was hot and pleasant for the dragons, with plentiful feed running through the forests. The heat of summer usually made the dragons lazier, but happier altogether. And despite the abundant availability of food, they also didn't need to eat as much in the summer.

When summer turned to autumn, leaves would change color and the coolness of winter could be felt in the air once more. Three moons in each season were enough for Dak, except in summer. As the frozen air stung his snout again, Dak's thoughts drifted back to his warm cave and the hot summer sun.

The surface world surrounding the Rock Clouds consisted mostly of thick forests. Dak had heard tales from other dragons of sweeping plains and treacherous oceans, but had yet to see any of them himself. His feelings alternated between anxiety and anticipation throughout the long, cold night.

As the first and largest of the moons neared the horizon, Dak saw in the distance a long break in the trees, as if a godly hand had clawed the earth clear. He put on a burst of speed when he realized he could see better because the first rays of sunlight illuminated the sky. He feared that if he didn't catch up to his friends tonight, he never would.

He surged his wings as stars began to disappear. When he reached the opening in the forest line, he saw a smaller river running between the trees. Centaur River was at least as wide as four fully grown dragons standing head to tail. But this river was only as wide as one dragon and could be easily crossed. Dak scanned ahead for the seven dragons he followed when movement on the edge of the river, almost below him now, caught his eye.

He squinted in the direction of the movement and saw both the happiest and the worst sight he'd ever seen. Six dragons lay curled on the rocky bank of the water; the seventh was presumably on watch. He immediately dropped his right wing and lifted his left almost straight up in the air. He spun in midair and dove wildly for the forest below. Once he could touch the treetops with his claws, he caught the air in his wings to slow himself. Being again out of visual range, Dak allowed himself to drop quietly to the forest floor.

Dak slipped through the trees with little to no sound, as there weren't many leaves to rustle in doing so. Stepping lightly, he waited in silence. He didn't hear dragon sounds, but he thought he caught the sound of wood scraping against wood. He tried to hold as still as the trees surrounding him until he heard the unmistakable sound of a footfall behind him. With his jaw opened in a silent snarl, he whipped his head around, only to find himself nose-to-nose with the tip of an arrow.

"By The One, Dragon!" the dark brown centaur lowered her weapon with the speed of a practiced hand. "You nearly scared me off my hooves!"

Dak closed his hanging jaw. "My apologies, mighty centaur." Once the quiver regained the arrow, Dak noticed the beauty of the one who had almost killed him. He knew her to be female because of the leather binding crossing her chest, but other than this difference male and female centaurs looked and acted very much alike. Probably because of the cold weather, she had a short fur wrapping around her shoulders, but most of her skin was exposed because centaur skin was thicker than that of a human or faerie. Her only other clothing was thick leather bracers on her fore-arms and the cannon bones of her legs. Around the barrel of her body were more leather bindings, but these contained pockets for supplies suggesting prac-ticality rather than modesty. Feathers, beads and col-orful threads adorned her black hair, which twisted into intricate interlacing braids from the top of her head all the way down her back and into her mane. Her eyes, three times as large as a human's, sparkled up at him, making him catch his breath slightly. "I wasn't aware of the need to announce myself."

"You're black as night!" the centaur grinned at him. "I would think you might be used to announcing yourself. I am Ashel," she said, touching the bridge of her nose with her right fingers, "Leader of the Warrior Centaurs."

Dak had been taught the centaur greeting and returned it clumsily. He first touched the top of his head (where a forehead might be), then he touched between his eyes. Then, placing his claw on his chest, he dipped his head to her. "I didn't know centaurs had warriors." The moment he said the words, he knew they would deem him a novice in the world outside of the Rock Clouds.

But the beautiful centaur woman winked at him. "I know most centaurs prefer to stargaze, but we each have our special talents."

"And what are yours?"

Ashel gazed up at him from under sweeping eye-lashes. "Sneaking up on dragons." Her kind smile added to her warmth. "Come, my friend. You're welcome here." The umber beauty trotted away, but called to Dak over her shoulder. "What's your name? Or should I just call you 'friend'?"

Dak knew the centaurs were friendly to all drag-ons, even those cast out of the rucks. But he thought he should still tread carefully. "My name is Dakoon Ido Tusten," he said as he followed her swishing tail.

Ashel waved a hand over her shoulder. The cen-taurs weren't friendly with the faeries, although they kept their reasons to themselves. "Don't spread that Faerie vulgarity here," she said. "What's your chosen name?"

"Dak."

"Much better, Dak," she said as she led on.

"Where are we going?" Dak asked, trying to take in his surroundings. The bleak forest encroached all around. Dak knew they marched closer to Priya and her contingent, but couldn't tell how far away they still might be.

"To your travel companions, of course."

"What?" Dak stopped in his tracks to scour the for-est. They weren't yet within sight of the contingent.

"What's the matter?" Ashel turned to examine him.

"They can't know I'm here."

"Ah," she nodded as realization lit her big eyes. "Rogue? Fugitive? Criminal?"

Dak's head hung. "All."

"Hmm." He raised his head to look in her eyes. "Well, I would never make a good leader if I didn't know how to keep secrets." She met Dak's stare with a half grin. She turned to look into the forest for a moment. With the silence, Dak heard the sound of more hooves. Ashel lifted her fingers to her lips and trilled a pealing note that sounded more like bells than a whistle. A moment later another brown centaur trotted into view. When he was almost a dragon's length away, Ashel lifted her hand. "Stop."

The centaur halted. His similarity in appearance to Ashel's was striking, with the same color of their horse's body and hair, but the new arrival was clearly male. He wore only a fur slung over his shoulders and the leather bindings on his legs. Instead of archers' bracers on his arms, he had leather thongs twisted from his wrists up his forearms and around the bulging muscles of his biceps and shoulders. Though he wore many more feathers in his hair, the effect wasn't as colorful. Another leather belt wrapped around his waist and crossed one way over his chest from hip to shoulder. Dak could see the hilt of a shining silver sword over his shoulder and the bottom of its leather sheath. Another simpler sword hung at his waist and several knives adorned the belt around his barrel. Although not the leader of the warriors, this centaur was not one to cross.

"What is it, Ashel?" the male asked, but his gaze swept Dak.

"This dragon," she stuck a thumb in Dak's direction, "is hiding from the others." The male nodded as if this happened every day. "Tell Joss I'll have to stay with him, since I already have his scent on me."

"Sure," said the male. "Do you need anything?"

"No, thanks," Ashel shook her head. "Just tell the guard to keep clear for now."

The other centaur gave the traditional greeting, touching his forehead, nose bridge and chest, and nodding his head; Ashel returned the gesture touching only the bridge of her nose. Then the male trotted off the same way he had come.

Ashel turned back to Dak. "My brother, Rylan." She jerked her head in the direction of the retreating centaur. "He's a good centaur. You can trust us, Dak."

"Thank you," he said as they started off again in the direction of the river. "Who is Joss?"

"Our eldest brother, Ruler of the Centaurs of Avonoa. Rylan is his personal protector."

"Ruler?" Dak questioned as he gathered his pace to follow again. "What are the Ruler of the Centaurs and the Leader of the Warrior Centaurs doing this far from home?" As far as he knew centaur herds spread out on the hilly plains surrounding Centaur River, but the Ruler of the Centaurs usually dwelt on the north side of the river near the White Ocean. He wondered what these, the highest ranking centaurs, might be doing so far from their base.

Ashel stopped for a moment to stare into the sky from between the tree branches. "Training," she answered. "Come," she said, resuming her pace. Dak peered up at the disappearing stars, wondering what she saw in them, then hurried to keep up with her.

She led the black dragon through the forest to a thicket of trees and large boulders, beyond which Dak could see the sun-dazzled banks of the river.

"Your friends are resting over there." Ashel pointed with her hand toward the sleeping dragons. "They shouldn't see, hear or smell you here."

"Thank you," he nodded to her again.

"Get some rest." She swept her hand toward the rocks. "You must be tired." As Dak dropped his weary body down for a long awaited rest, Ashel smiled. "I'll be back when you wake."

With these last words, Ashel dashed back into the forest. Dak's eyes drooped low. Closing his eyes, he could just make out the quiet conversation of the others.

They lay on the rocks next to the river, but none slept. "We're fortunate to have the centaurs' help," Priya told the others. "Rest well, now. Tomorrow we sleep in the Black Forest."

Dak could hear them adjusting their positions until Tog spoke up. "Tusten," he said in a low voice. "What's in the Black Forest?"

"There are many dark creatures, which humans fear," Dak's father answered. "However, there are no creatures dragons fear."

"Are there scorrands?" Tog asked.

"Scorrands, lydik, horses, eagles," Tusten answered, his voice muffled by what Dak assumed was his claws resting over his snout.

"What about banshees?" Tog asked with what sounded to Dak like a little trepidation. This was, after all, his first time on the surface world as well.

"Yes," came Priya's sharp whisper. "A great many number of creatures reside in the Black Forest. Now, please, rest while you can." Dak's question had been answered. Miraculously, no one had seen him, despite his carelessness. He grinned to himself at his cleverness and quickly fell asleep.

6

Tabulations

Philip's boots pounded in rhythm as he tromped over the ground inside Kingstor castle. He crossed the inner courtyard with its crisp brown grass to the doors leading out to the square. Normally he addressed the citizens of the kingdom from the royal balcony overlooking the courtyard and square, but this time he would be overlooking his guards and the two faeries before they left on a most dangerous mission. He felt he should be in front of them personally. These small differences between him and his father would set his reign apart should his father's health fail.

But when the guards at the gate opened the doors, Philip saw three lines of ten men waiting, but no faeries. Rage swelled in his heart, but he had been well trained in hiding emotion. General Bragon sat atop his black stallion at the side of the men.

"Where are the faeries?" Philip asked his general.

"They have not –" Bragon started, but stopped when a hum met everyone's ears.

The two faeries drifted lazily over the road leading to the magnificent square. Philip stood his ground, making them come to him.

When they finally greeted him, he simply said "In the future, you will be ready to go on time. Do I make myself clear?"

"We are on time, Sire," Kradik answered, then swept his hand toward the men. "We are now entirely prepared to leave."

Philip stared over the top of Kradik's cowl. "It is the custom in the Noble Kingdom that the ruler need be the last person present for any gathering." Philip had been taught to assert his position when he addressed the citizens of his kingdom by casting his gaze above their eyes, either at their forehead or over their head. He showed preference to only a few dozen people by looking them directly in the eye, but never a servant, staff-guard or commoner. He usually met eyes with nobles and foreign visitors such as faeries, so he hoped his gaze over the top of Kradik's head would send him a message.

"We shall not forget," Kradik answered as the two faeries bowed.

Philip hoped this beginning wasn't an indication of how his decision to accept the faeries' help would turn out. "Bragon!" he called. General Bragon turned his horse toward the prince. "Do what you can to scare the dragons, but keep the men as far from harm as possible. There's no need –"

"You can't just scare away dragons!" Kradik cut him off.

Philip narrowed his eyes at the faerie. "That is the second time you have interrupted me, Kradik." He spoke every word slowly. "The next time will be your last." Speaking loudly so everyone could hear, but keeping his eyes on the faerie's head, he said, "You will fire upon the dragons to steer them from their course. Capture them if possible, but lethal force will NOT be necessary. While you are in my kingdom, I am your liege lord. If you do not show the respect my station demands, your head will be sent back to your Faerie Council with my compliments!"

"It is not your kingdom, yet...My Liege," Kradik answered in a whisper.

"I am the crown prince here, Kradik," he lowered his voice again. "If you assist, you will do as I command." He knew from Bragon's instruction that he must assert his authority over the faeries sooner rather than later. Even though it didn't come naturally to him, he had practiced it often.

After a moment of what Philip could only assume was burning anger shooting from their eyes, the two faeries withdrew from in front of the men to stand beside the formation. Philip took it as a symbol they were ready to assume their rightful position within his ranks. They stayed. This was most important as they were the only ones able to protect his men from slaughter.

"Sire," Bragon jumped down from his horse. "What will we do with a dragon if we should capture any?"

"I've no idea," Philip said only to his general, "but I couldn't allow them to dictate to me, now could I?"

Bragon jumped back into his saddle with a grin on his face. Clenching his fist to his chest in salute, he said, "I'm proud to serve you, My Liege." The salute symbolized the king's guards' oath of willingness to lay down their life for their ruler. Philip knew that Bragon, of all people, would be most willing to do so.

Throughout Philip's life, General Bragon had been not just the general in charge of the royal family's safety and overseeing the king's guards in the castle, but he had also been a trusted advisor and friend. He had taught Philip all he knew about battle, strategy and politics since he was a young child. Philip still had regular practice sessions with the general and some of his men. Though suddenly Philip felt a pang of reluctance to send his mentor on this mission, he knew that he would have to give much more difficult orders throughout his reign.

Philip stepped back to allow Bragon to lead the men and the faeries out of the square. With a yell to his men, they saluted their prince the same way then turned to follow the general. As the men beat a marching pace on the cobbled stones, Bragon yelled back to the prince. "You'll hear word of us in three days' time!"

7

Divine Stars

The sun hid behind a sheet of gray sky, making the forest feel even colder, if that was possible. Dak itched to roll out of his hiding place and find a nice warm spot in the sun, but he'd have to go very far to find it. If any of the group found him, they would know he had gone against Rakgar's orders and was therefore a traitor - not to be spoken to. Even if he went back to the Rock Clouds now, he wouldn't be allowed to speak in Rakgar's presence, and no one in the ruck would be allowed to speak to him. Usually, only brave or loyal friends will speak to a traitor dragon or help them, even if they're innocent. If they're caught consorting with the traitor they can be punished, although it might be a lesser sentence. Perhaps a moon of exile or so.

Under normal circumstances, a dragon who disobeyed Rakgar's orders would be banished from the Rock Clouds. Depending upon the severity of the infraction, the length of banishment would vary. In this case, Dak could not be banished because he had not passed The Krusible. The only punishment left for such an action is death. Dak knew he could never go back to the Rock Clouds. He would likely be hunted by his own friends and family for the rest of his life. But if he could pass the Krusible in the desert, perhaps he could someday go back to make amends. If he could convince a dragon close to him – maybe his father or even Tog – to speak for him, Rakgar might forgive his trespass. Whoever might speak for him would receive the same punishment as Dak, but at this point, a year or two of banishment on the surface with his father or Tog didn't seem so bad.

Dak awoke before his friends. He wondered where Ashel had gone while he slept, but he didn't have to wonder long. She soon trotted into view with something slung over her horse back.

"You're awake!" she said as she stopped next to him. Reaching behind her, she dropped a large boar in front of him. "I've been hunting." Indicating the kill, she said, "Help yourself."

The sky over head had crept into darkness again, but the clouds departed leaving a scintillating clear overhead. Dak worried the others would leave without him noticing. He threw a curious glance their way.

"Don't worry," Ashel answered his unspoken question. "They'll be eating with Joss. It's centaur etiquette to dine with your guests before they depart."

As she said it, Dak watched a few centaurs trot into view of the riverbank with similar offerings for the other dragons.

"Have you eaten?" Dak asked Ashel before he filled his mouth.

Ashel touched the bridge of her nose again, saying, "Yes, thank you," before she bent her knees to sit next to him on the ground.

"Why do you salute that way?" he asked between bites. "I thought all centaurs gave the traditional salute."

Ashel grinned. "Do you know what our greeting means?"

Dak shrugged as he ripped off a limb. "Something about watching the future, present and past?"

"Close." She touched her forehead. "'Be mindful of the future,'" she recited; then she touched the bridge of her nose, "'see to the present;'" then, touching her chest, she finished, "'and never regret the past.' The warrior centaurs," she told him, "are always mindful of the future and hope to live to never regret the past, but our foremost duty is to concentrate on the present.

"While other centaurs focus on reading our futures in the stars, we are bound to protect and serve our people in the here and now. We 'see to the present,' so this is our salute."

"Can you still read the stars, like others?"

Ashel giggled, a tinkly musical sound. "All centaur children are taught to master the stars, their movements and their meanings. Even if later in life we decide not to practice it as much as others, we never forget it."

"Could you tell my future by the stars?" Dak asked. Nothing was left of his boar but ribs and some bits of wealth.

"It's not that simple." She smiled again and looked up into the sky. The trees overhead didn't afford a great view of the night sky, but they could see a few stars. "Do you see that star there?" she pointed. "Above that branch? The beautiful orange one?"

"I think so, but they all look the same color to me."

She smiled at him. "I forget that dragons see the stars in the same colorless way humans do." She turned back to the stars. "We centaurs can see them in many brilliant colors."

"If I saw them that way," Dak said gazing up. "I would watch the stars more often as well, I think."

"The orange star is my favorite," Ashel continued, "so it represents me and my journey in life. I can see other stars it will intercept on its path. This gives me an idea of what I might experience ahead."

Dak gazed into the twinkling little specks of light wondering how she could interpret her life ahead. "But centaurs can often interpret the stars for others. How do you do that?"

"I don't pretend to hold the gifts of others, Dak." She shook her head. "There are many things seen in the stars. Sometimes they hold true. Sometimes we misread the stars. But," she narrowed her eyes at him, "I think I might've noticed your star a few nights ago."

Shifting her large eyes back to the sky, she studied them for a moment. "Normally," she said as she twisted her neck back and forth searching the sky through the trees, "I would have to watch your star for at least a few nights to see which path it might take, and the stars around it to see how they might interact with each other. But I noticed yours, seeing that ours would intercept, so I might be able to..." her voice trailed off as she read the stars. Dak swallowed the last of the boar while he waited for her to speak.

Eventually, the grin slid from her face. "Yours is a dark star," she pointed to one near her own, "next to mine, just as our paths have converged now. It's dark, but different..." She swept her finger in one direction first, then another, in a V-shape. "Mine will go this way, as far as I can tell, yours will go another way." She grinned at him again. "But we'll meet again soon and it seems our paths might even run together for a while."

"We'll travel together?"

"Travel, perhaps." she shrugged, "or perhaps simply work toward the same goal."

Dak nodded. "I can live with that."

Ashel's smile slipped again as her eyes lifted back to the stars. "Unfortunately, what lies in your immediate path isn't as pleasant."

Dak's forehead creased in concern. "What is it?"

"There are two stars representing faeries you'll meet. Soon." With these words she reached out and placed a hand on Dak's claw. "I know centaurs say this too often, but Dak, please believe me, the faeries are not to be trusted."

"What have they done now?" Centaurs and faeries had long been enemies, although neither would explain the cause. Many dragons shared numerous stories of faeries and centaurs complaining about the other.

Ashel straightened her back. "Hear me out." She fingered her bowstring stretched across her chest. "We came across two faeries a few weeks ago. We kept our distance, never making our presence known. It was rather difficult for some of us." She turned her big brown eyes up to him again. "But we heard part of their conversation. Dak, they said they're working on a dragon toxin. They said it could render a fully grown dragon unconscious in an instant!"

"But," he shook his head, "the faeries have always been our allies, as much as the centaurs."

"Their stars have trails of bitterness behind them."

"Bitterness from what?"

"I don't know." Her eyes bored into his. "But you must be careful."

Dak tried to move past the subject. "What else do you see that I might encounter?"

Ashel sighed but returned her gaze to the sky. "There's another star after the faeries', if you make it past them, that seems just as dangerous. Another creature of some sort."

"How can you tell it's dangerous?"

"Danger," she told him, "is evident in the number of rays a star emits. This one has several."

"Sounds like fun." He saw nothing remarkable in the little dots winking down at him. "Anything else?"

"At many different times ahead, you'll be surrounded by humans. It's almost as if they're converging on you. Cold will threaten you. And you'll also be influenced by – " she winked at him, "the Star of Love."

"All this and your most adamant warning is about two faeries?"

"At least we know what they're about," she said.

"Some would say that makes them less dangerous, not more."

She pursed her lips at him, but allowed the corners of her mouth to curl up. "Possibly." She turned to look toward the river. "But tonight, you'll fly."

Dak saw the riverbank was empty. He didn't know how much lead the contingent had, but he knew he should leave quickly.

Ashel stood and Dak stood next to her. "Our stars will cross paths again, Dak." She saluted him again in farewell. "Until we meet again, may your star shine bright."

Dak offered her the three-tiered salute he knew before she galloped away into the forest. He watched her swishing tail disappear behind the trees, then turned his attention to the chase.

He crawled out from the prickly bushes to stretch his back and neck. He flexed his claws, enjoying the feel of the dirt as he dug it between his talons. He walked to the river's edge where his friends had been and opened his wings. The colder air by the icy water made it difficult to get lift. He labored against the air, but he didn't want to be seen, so he lifted himself only enough to peer over the trees. Ahead in the dark he could barely make out the group as they flew over the Black Forest.

When the contingent was far enough ahead, he lifted himself above the trees. While he flew he watched the group carefully. He thought he could see Tog and Tusten in the back of a circle formation now. The youngest and least experienced with the oldest and most experienced. They would alternate taking turns checking the sky and ground behind them. As the moons rose above the trees, Dak was happy to see three crescents. They didn't give off enough light to manifest him at this distance.

Even with the scant light, Dak thought he saw Tog drop behind the group and hover. Dak tucked his wings and fell into the trees below. He knew Tog might have seen him, but hoped to have escaped any lingering gaze. He ran along in the murky forest trying not to think of what might be watching him, but knowing he couldn't risk flying for the moment. As soon as he came to a clearing, he took to the air again.

As the slender moons crossed the sky, Dak thought he might have been spotted again. He dropped into the trees a second time only to find his path blocked by a scorrand, a giant two-headed lizard. Normally, these creatures acted like any earth-bound lizard – lazy, slow, unintelligent and unaggressive – but this one bared its dagger-sharp teeth and hissed at Dak with both heads. He backed away slowly until his back claw stumbled over something round. Dak's heart sank as he heard a loud crack underfoot. His claw grasped something soft and wet. He turned for a moment to see if his assumption was correct. He had just squashed an egg, with more nearby in a nest of stones.

Tusten had taught Dak many important things when he was a hatchling. One of them was never come between a parent and their young. If he had broken an egg, nowhere would be far enough away for Dak to run now. His only hope of escape would be to kill the mother. "I guess I'll get something more to eat sooner rather than later," he mumbled to himself guiltily.

Scorrands were not much of a threat except for their size. This one stood taller than Rakgar with both necks stretched over her, although her body wasn't as large. The trees in the Black Forest were twice the size of this creature, and as thick around as his own body, but Dak would not be able to gain flight from their branches because their canopies grew together so closely at the top.

The scorrand hissed again and advanced. Dak tried to side-step it. He thought about crouching low, but realized the beast could step on him and end it. So he jumped to a tree trunk, latching onto it with his claws.

He used his tail to swipe at one head while slashing at the second with his left claw. He opened his maw to burn the beast with fire, but realized his mistake before he did. If he loosed any flame, the contingent would see it. Expecting some other dragon, they would find him. He would have to do this without fire.

The darkness didn't help him. Scorrands can see in the dark with their huge, nocturnal eyes, so she had Dak at a disadvantage there as well. Her heads took turns snapping at the black intruder until she batted him from the tree with her large front claw. Dak slid across the forest floor on all fours with three gashes in his right shoulder. The heads continued their tirade while the front claws swatted her prey. She hit Dak four times before he escaped to her side.

Before she could turn completely to confront him, he clawed her across her rear haunches, but forgot about her tail. Her legs flinched, but she let her tail fly. He saw it from the corner of his eye before it hurled him into another tree trunk, this time buffeting one of his wings and his head. He lay dazed on the forest floor for a moment. Then he thought of his friends. If he didn't get away from this beast, he might lose them. He gathered his strength.

He growled while crouching low to the ground, and realized this should have been his first move. When she lifted her front foot to stomp on him, Dak shot under her belly. His claws dug deep into her flesh at the soft point where her legs met her body. He knew it to be a weak spot for dragons and assumed it would be for this creature as well. With a scream, she reared to back off, but his teeth met the joint of her two necks. She latched onto him with both front feet and ripped him away, but to her detriment. He brought a chunk of her chest with him.

Dark red blood painted the forest floor between them like a black shadow spreading rapidly across the ground. The beast languidly snapped at the black dragon with one of her heads, but he easily batted it away. Her body crashed to the ground in a pool of her own blood. With a gurgle then a moan, she lay still.

The only time Dak had ever made his own kill had been as a hatchling when his mother taught him to hunt and stalk. She had brought a couple of rabbits to a little valley for him to practice. He remembered his heart beating hard in his chest, but it hadn't compared to the elation he now felt. That had been fun. This was pure exhilaration!

He felt hot blood coursing through his body as he watched the life slip out of his victim. His heart felt like it attacked him from the inside. Crazed with blood lust, he stared at his enemy then opened his mouth wider than his head with the joy of his kill. But he choked to strangle the exultant bellow that almost escaped him as he remembered not to reveal himself. Dak clamped his eyes shut and took a deep breath to quiet the fighting fury rising in him.

When he had calmed enough, he limped to the back of the creature. Using his teeth and claws, he tore off her tail. He had felt its power and didn't know when he would eat again otherwise. He carried it with him as he staggered away from the remains.

Instead of searching for a clearing, Dak climbed a tree. It took him three sore limps before he could tear away branches at the top. Carefully perching atop the trees, he opened his wings to catch the air. With the scorrand tail in his front claws, he flew in the direction of the mountains again.

His shoulder felt painfully cold as he lifted into the air, like claws of ice slicing over it in waves. Cold was never a good sign for a dragon. His left wing had cushioned him against the tree in his struggle with the scorrand and now felt worse than when Visi had helped him escape. The cold ache dulled after a while, but the wing joint began to sting. However, Dak's determination forced him to press on.

As he flew, Dak devoured the scorrand tail. Although the tail slowed him along with his injuries, he felt sure of his direction and hoped the extra energy reserves would outweigh the speed lost. Most dragons preferred to eat burnt flesh, but raw served just as well, if one could stomach it. Eventually, he dropped the scraps into the forest below. The freshly eaten meat gave Dak extra fire in his belly to try to heal himself. Once he could discern Priya and the others in front of him once more, he dropped to the forest floor. He used his left claw to hide the small but intense flame as he passed it carefully over his shoulder wounds. Healing oneself didn't work as well as healing another dragon with fire, but it did as much as licking the wound, bringing a small amount of relief.

Dak pressed on as best he could through the night. He followed Priya's contingent unless someone appeared to see him, at which point he would drop into the trees and follow on foot. But before too long he would find a clearing and take to the sky again. The other dragons, however, never stopped. But having seven in the company, their pace remained slow and steady.

Dak was forced to hide in the trees eight times in the night, but he refused to give up his quest. Eventually the sky began to gleam at the horizon. As the group in front of him dropped, Dak did the same, grateful for the coming rest.

He didn't bother to catch up to the group before he slept. He assumed they would leave once the sun fell again. On a full stomach, he would rest easy through the day and be better healed in order to set out behind the group that night. Dragons healed quickly. Often, with minor injuries, they could heal over a full stretch of sleep. More serious injuries might take a few sun cycles to heal. Having to fight the algid temperatures meant his body wouldn't heal as quickly, but he comforted himself with the thought that flying would get easier over the nights to come. He would not allow a few scrapes to dissuade him.

8

Revelations

Dak had no idea what woke him. One second, he slept peacefully in the dim light of day in the Black Forest. The next, his eyes were open, peering into the shadows around him. Something was out there. He lay perfectly still. He even stopped breathing for a few moments.

Light dappled the forest floor around him, but the Black Forest had been given its name for a reason. The trees were so thick even without leaves the light had trouble peeking through the branches. With no way to tell, Dak assumed the sun hung near the middle of the sky. But without sufficient light, he was well hidden on the forest floor.

His experience with the scorrand made him realize the dangers in this forest. Huntresses liked to hunt in the Black Forest with its numerous large creatures. In one trip they could feed many dragons. But the risk often outweighed the benefits. Dak's mother had died here.

Dak lay silent, barely breathing, but nothing happened. He silently cursed Tog and his apprehensions for tainting his own courage. With a sigh, he closed his eyes.

Stupid superstitions, he thought to himself.

With his eyes closed and the world once again dark, Dak heard a twig snap. This time he kept his eyes shut. It was nothing, he told himself.

A shuffling of leaves met his ears. Stop trying to scare yourself, he growled in his own mind.

"Dakoon." The voice was no more than a soft breeze on the wind. This time he not only opened his eyes, but jumped to his feet with fangs bared.

Before him stood a woman. Golden curls fell down her back and over her bare shoulders. She wore a plain white dress bound with a single golden cord around her waist, but the simple effect increased her beauty, even to a dragon. She had a small, pointed chin and long neck at the bottom of her oval face. Full lips and high cheekbones complimented slightly tilted eyes. She stood less than a dragon's length away from him, but she harbored no fear in her eyes. On the contrary, her brow creased in concern over her piercing blue eyes.

"I know you will not ask who I am or where I come from, so I will tell you." Her soft voice drifted on the winter breeze to him. "My name is Annette and I come from the World of Souls."

Dragons and most other intelligent beings believed that when anyone died the soul departed the body to dwell in another layer of the world around them, unseen by the living. All species referred to this as the World of Souls. At times the souls could make themselves known and even communicate with the corporeal world. Dragons passed on stories of loved ones visiting them or helping them at times of need, but there was no way to know how or when a soul would appear. Although seemingly solid, Dak knew this woman to be one of these souls because she had no scent. Besides, if she was human, she would freeze in the thin material of the dress she wore. But who she was or how she knew him, he couldn't answer.

"Dakoon," she repeated, "You must go to your friend, now," she said with conviction. But Dak remained still. The woman cast her eyes to the ground, then walked past Dak and continued in the direction he had come.

Dak watched her walk away with only his eyes not daring to twitch. He noticed her bare feet stepped silently over the brown leaves and left no footprint when she tread on a small patch of frost. He realized he must have sensed her presence before she appeared, but the sounds weren't her own. When she left his vision a gentle breeze swept through the area. The wind repeated her last word, "now."

Dak bent his neck to see if the woman continued her address, but she was gone. Dak thought for a moment an ice cold squirrel had scampered up his back, but he allowed himself a shiver then immediately set off in the direction of Priya and her contingent.

His wounds remained only partially healed. He was sore and tired, but he forced himself on among the trees. A fresh wave of fatigue attacked him as he tromped through the forest, but he knew the woman, Annette – whoever she was – wouldn't have spoken to him unless it was important. So he pressed on. The sky became laden with gray clouds, making the forest even darker despite the distant sun. Dak's head hung in front of him as he walked.

As his nose lagged along next to the ground, Dak focused on the different smells of the beasts in the Black Forest. He caught the tangy scent of the scorrand, but many scents presented themselves for which Dak had no reference. Every beast he could detect with his sensitive nose had passed this way a long time ago. Until …

Dak stopped. A strong scent lay across his path. It was fresh. He pulled at it with his nostrils. It smelled of winter even more so than the air around him. Cold. Dirt. But it also had a soft smell, like powder-fresh snow, mixed with the woody scent of the trees. Something that lived in the trees. Anything cold was an enemy to a dragon, and some creatures existed that even dragons couldn't fight. This scent, he could associate to one creature through the memories passed to him by his mother. A banshee.

The banshee scream was deadly to anyone in its path, but only at close quarters. It could fly, but only short distances. In fact, it looked and acted like a large black bird, roosting in trees and laying eggs in nests. It was smaller than a dragon, but still a dangerous foe, with sharp claws and a long beak.

Dak followed the banshee's scent. It wasn't on the ground long. His keen nose followed it into a tree. Then to another. And another. He needed only a few moments to recognize its path. It headed for Priya's contingent.

Dak followed on foot as fast as he could, trying to keep as silent as possible. Normally dans can't sneak up on a forgant, the most dim-witted, fuzzy creature the gods could create. But Dak's acute senses gave him grace other dans admired without words. He hurried along, leaping from shadow to shadow in the chance the banshee might see him. He knew his course following the creature was correct because he would intermittently pick up its fresh scent. He just hoped he wouldn't be too late.

Before long he could just make out the group of dragons in the distance, so he slowed. They nestled at the bottom of a slight depression. He knew at least one dragon would be on watch, possibly two. He doubted if Priya would have more than two of them stay awake at a time. Dak found a thick clump of tree trunks that grew in a tangled mass on the flank overlooking the group. He wriggled himself quietly into the branches.

At first glance, all seemed quiet. The contingent was well over ten dragon lengths away. He could easily watch them and remain hidden. He could see Priya in the middle of the clearing below him, the soft light making her green scales seem even more fulgent. Tusten lay next to her along with three others. They all lay breathing heavily, in a deep sleep.

Dak forced his eyes to penetrate the gloom beyond the group, looking for the two guards. He saw nothing but shadow. He readjusted his eyes to search the forest directly around him. He had to find whoever might be on guard. He searched the branches of the trees. Still nothing. Tog had talents he had never given his friend credit for.

As he searched the trees for any sign of dragon guards, he also searched for any sign of the banshee. He knew the banshee dropped from the treetops to attack. He also knew that only the banshee's prey would hear the fatal cry. He must locate them before it was too late.

Then he saw it. In the darkness where the branches bound together to form a thatch, one stick had stripes across it. As he watched, those stripes disappeared in waves to move down the limb. He knew they were the talons of the banshee, but Dak had to strain his eyes to make them believe it. He could barely make out a long orange beak somewhere above the lines on the branch. But the beak seemed to be turned down as if the beast peered at something. But Dak had searched those trunks and branches. He hadn't seen either of the two missing dragons there. Yes, there had been a spot his eyes seemed to be drawn to, but nothing was there except an odd tail-shaped branch.

The creature was close. Dak pondered attacking it to keep it away from the other dragons. Would they know? Would they hear? Would the dragon on guard notice? Perhaps two black creatures of the Black Forest wrestling in the branches wouldn't be of much concern to a group of traveling dragons.

Dak couldn't see anything more. He closed his eyes in frustration, thus allowing his other senses to take over. He could smell the seven dragons, each with their own unique scent. One of them was far away. He could smell Tog strongest. He was close. He must be the one on guard closest to Dak.

Careful to stay quiet, Dak pulled air into his nose, then held his breath. He could hear the sound of his own heart beating. Faintly, he could hear the sound of the banshee's heart beating. Its heart beat much faster than the other dragon's heart he could hear. Tog had to be near the creature. Dak forced himself to keep his eyes closed and listen. He heard the soft rustle of feathers. Talons scraping wood.

Dak shot from the trees as the banshee landed in front of Tog. Dak didn't see him until he stared wide-eyed at the beast in front of him. The banshee opened its mouth to deliver the attack, but Dak tackled it out of the trees. His jaw closed around its throat before they hit the ground. With a crunch and a stomp, the fight was over before it started. But the noise had awoken the others.

Tog landed on the ground behind Dak, who turned to face him, but kept his body as close to the ground as possible. Tog unabashedly stared with a slack maw and one dilated eye at Dak. He shook his head slowly as Tusten and Pantar rushed toward them. Dak chanced a quick glance over the rise at the two dragons closing in, then inspected his friend's face. Tog's eye swiveled to the ground then back up at Dak. He snapped his gaping mouth shut. Then with pursed lips, Tog jerked his head in the direction of the forest beyond.

Dak only had time to plunge behind some prickly bushes in the blackness before his father and Pantar crested the rise to join Tog. "What happened?" Tusten demanded in a low voice.

Tog scooped up the banshee in his mouth and tossed the carcass to his companions. "Banshee," he spat.

Tusten puffed out his chest. "Well done, Toggil," he nodded. "I'll inform Priya."

Pantar brought the remains with them as they returned to the camp, leaving Tog alone once more. When they were gone, Dak came out of his hiding place.

"You fool," Tog growled low. "What have you done?"

"Just saved your skinny neck, you ungrateful worm," Dak whispered back low enough to not be overheard.

"I should rather have died in the service of Priya than watch you continue to throw your life away," Tog said, meeting his friend's eyes. "Have you completely returned your mind to the faeries?"

Dak knew he would be upset. He just didn't know if Tog would turn him in or not. "I couldn't just sit there," he finally answered.

Tog burrowed one eye into Dak's. "You don't get it," Tog stretched his neck over to his friend. Putting his nose directly in front of Dak, he blew a memory into his face.

In an instant, Dak was transported back to Rakgar's cave. Rakgar paced back and forth across the hard floor, his claws clacking with every step.

"I fear his reaction to my punishment," he said.

"What can he do?" Tusten's voice came from Dak's point of view, so it must have been his memory. "He must follow orders."

Rakgar ceased his march. "Tusten, I'm afraid he'll flee." He continued tromping across the ground. "Then I'll be forced to hunt him down and have him killed."

The cave rang with the repetitive clacking. "No," Tusten offered, leaving his next thought unspoken.

Rakgar stopped again, but the question in his eyes gave way to understanding. Shaking his massive head, he said, "No!" He glared sternly at Tusten. "You can't!" he responded, but Tusten interrupted him.

"I'll bear my son's disgrace," Tusten announced clearly.

"Don't do this, Tusten!" Rakgar roared.

"If Dakoon should flee the Rock Clouds, I'll join him in exile to spare his life."

Dak blinked as he returned to himself in the dank forest. His knees sank to the ground. He stared blankly at Tog as his friend backed away.

"You have doomed your father as well as yourself," he whispered.

"I didn't know." Dak could barely speak.

"But you had a choice," Tog said firmly. "Now," his jaw worked his teeth together, "your only choice is whether to go back and be accountable, or allow your father to suffer in your stead."

The two friends sat in silence, unable to look at each other. Dak cowered behind a thick tree to keep hidden. As they pondered the predicament Dak had thrust on them, they heard Priya get up to move towards Tog.

"Go," he whispered. "This is the last act I can do as your friend." Dak searched his eye but found no hope. "Go, now, Dakoon. And I shall never see you again."

Dak disappeared into his covert before Priya could see him. His heart felt heavy. He wanted to scream at the sun more than when he had killed the scorrand, but the rage wrapped its fingers around his throat to smother him. He balled his claws up trying to resist the urge to break every tree within reach, then splayed them out and dug them silently into the frozen earth beneath him. Gaining control, Dak forced himself to lay silently on the forest floor as Priya approached Tog.

"Well done, Toggil," she hailed him. "You might have saved more lives than just your own."

Tog hung his head as if in humility while Dak watched from between the bushes. "Don't make it more than it is. I saved my own hide. Nothing more."

Priya grinned. "Humility does not become you, Toggil." But she peered closer at her friend. "What's wrong? You should be overcome with blood rush after your first kill."

"Perhaps I handle my rush differently," he said as he shrugged a shoulder.

"Congratulations, all the same," she said then turned to leave. But after just a step she turned back to face the gray dragon. "Tog, I won't lie to you. I know what's bothering you." Tog snapped an eye to meet hers and held his breath. "You're worried about Dakoon." As Tog tried to hide his relief, she continued. "He'll succeed despite himself, Toggil. Have faith in him." Dak ground his teeth together at her words.

Tog bared his teeth at Dak's bushes. "I fear there's no longer any hope for him."

9

Ambush

Dak spent the rest of the day tossing restlessly in a pile of soggy leaves melted from his heat as a few white flakes fell from the sky. When the sky darkened further, Dak still debated whether to follow Priya's group or not. The edge of the Black Forest was only a partial day's flight away. Beyond this, the trees rose with the land into the ever looming Torthoth Mountains. Dak assumed the desert waited on the other side, although he hadn't been able to see the landscape beyond. He tried to convince himself that he had not come so far only to return to the Rock Clouds and thereby not only lose his own freedom but also his father's.

Perhaps, he thought to himself, it might be best to continue on with my plan.

He assumed a day's flight through the mountains would bring him to the justice of the Desert Ruck. Hoping they might be more lenient than returning to face Rakgar, Dak set his mind to continue on. If only to make sure Priya and her contingent got to the Desert Ruck safely.

Dak waited in the darkening forest much longer than on previous nights. Before, he had been excited and anxious. Now, as he grappled with his guilt, time slipped away. In his black attitude, the creatures avoided him. Eventually, the clouds disappeared, the stars shone and the judgmental moons threw a ray through the trees at a slight angle to help him realize he had tarried too long.

With another roll of his shoulder, he trudged again through the forest. Finally lifting into the air, Dak almost hoped he wouldn't catch up to the group. Maybe they would slip away from him and he would be lost forever in the Black Forest.

The Torthoth Mountains glistened in the moonlight with a fresh veil of white. He knew from his mother's memories that the Torthoth Mountains resembled the Rock Clouds, with a multitude of plant and animal species, but they reached so far into the sky that even dragons had difficulty flying over them. He'd heard some humans thought the gods themselves lived at the top, watching happenings from above. But the dragons who had reached the heights found nothing there but stunted shrubbery.

Even for dragons to climb such heights was no mean feat. The thin air wasn't strong enough to fuel the fire in a dragon's belly, and they needed to eat many times along the way to make their fire remain bright. No one knew how Visi stayed alive, especially for as long as she had, at the top of the Inner Mountain which dwarfed the Torthoth Range. Flying over low clouds during rainstorms and between the mountain valleys posed no problems, but climbing over the Torthoth Mountains or to the top of the Inner Mountain took strength of mind and body.

Still stiff and slightly battered, Dak skirted between the lower mountain elevations. Looking back, he noticed the top of the Black Forest covered in the same layer of white as the mountains.

Luckily for Dak, even without his extra sensory perception, dragons had an excellent sense of direction. They know the compass points without any references, no matter how unfamiliar the territory. When the Black Forest disappeared behind the first mountain peaks, he continued on the proper course across the range.

He continued on through the night, inwardly struggling to justify his decision. How could he persuade the Desert Rakdar to allow him to test in their next Krusible? Would it even be worth it? When would he reveal himself to Priya and the others? Perhaps the Desert Rakdar would order Dak killed when she heard his story and Rakgar wouldn't have to sentence his father to anything. The different scenarios he played in his mind quickly turned ugly. The consequences of his actions would be devastating to all.

The Torthoth Mountain range ran only six summits deep, so Dak soon saw an exit to the landscape beyond. He landed on a rock outcrop overlooking the view, but still within the mountain range. The memories of the Desert Ruck told their mountain home to be surrounded by hot, barren desert for miles on every side, thus protecting them from intrusion by humans or any other surface creatures. All dragon rucks used natural resources to protect themselves from the humans. The Desert Ruck used barren desert, the Island Ruck used water, the Iceland Ruck used miles of frozen wastes and the Rock Cloud Ruck used height.

However, rather than desert, the landscape Dak saw beyond these mountains had just as many forests and rivers and lakes as the terrain he had just crossed. His disappointment at the view in front of him felt like an icy claw wrapped around his stomach. A stretch of what appeared to be frozen grasslands or plains lay to the left and a large teardrop-shaped body of water lay to his right. He couldn't see much else in the dark, but he knew the Desert Ruck was nowhere near.

Groaning inwardly at his own assumptions, Dak peered into the obsidian horizon to find Priya and Tog. He could see nothing. He closed his eyes and took a deep breath. As he sat in silence, his other senses overtook him again. He smelled smoke. Wood burning and food cooking smoke. Humans or faeries must be nearby. He heard the crack of a tree, and then a growl. That was a dragon!

Dak's eyes popped open, but he kept in tune with his other senses. Swiveling his head to discern where the sounds came from, he heard men yelling. The clink of metal. Another growl. Another sharp snap. They were around the bend of the mountain, slightly in front of him to his right. Not far at all.

He launched himself into the air and heaved the stinging wind back as hard as he could. The wind picked up as if to delay him longer. Dak dropped his right wing to circle the remaining portion of the mountain. Every wingfall felt like a lifetime. As he finally rounded the mountain from where the noises emanated, the smell of wood fire filled his nostrils and mingled with the bitter scent of blood. His stomach lurched when he recognized the smells.

At first, all he could see was a few fires clinging stubbornly to blackened tree trunks. Smoke from the burning branches tickled him with a faint warmth he wished he could stop to enjoy. But he could still hear movement farther away. Human men talking. If he closed his eyes, he could hear them dragging something large. He immediately thought of chasing the men down, but his disgust of the species stopped him. He justified his choice by thinking that he must avoid conflict so he could search for traces of survivors.

He landed as silently as possible in the middle of the worst of the scorch marks. The crackling flames annoyed him, so pressing his lips to the burning wood, he drew in a heavy breath. He could taste the familiar scent of his father in the flames. The second and third fires held the scent of Pantar.

Why would the contingent use their fire against humans? The humans must have attacked them. Dak had often been taught that humans will attack for no reason. The contingent must have flown over a human camp and the humans found sport in killing them. But Priya would never allow them to fight because of a senseless attack.

His eyes swept the ground hungrily, but his nose found his first clue. He could smell the stink of the fluids draining from human skin; 'sweat', they called it, or so he'd heard. Humans were filthy. He tried to ignore the stench and put his useless eyes to work.

Only a thin layer of snow covered the mountain floor, but it had been beaten down by the footprints of human boots. The boots appeared to dance around a pile of smoldering embers which lay next to a charred human skeleton. Dak could smell the scent of Kikum on the embers. At least he had taken one of the humans with him to the World of Souls. He hung his head for a moment in remembrance of his fallen friend, then continued his search for the others.

More boot prints mingled with dragon tracks. The dragon tracks smelled of Garmod and Tog. They circled another mangled human body, its vivid red blood threw an ominous contrast with the pure white snow, a broken bow at his side and a quiver of arrows spilled around him. The oddly metallic scent of the splattered blood reminded Dak of the Rock Clouds, but not quite. He listened intently, but none of their hearts beat.

Members of both species were dead. Dak knew the dragons would not have been the first to attack; dragons would only have killed the humans if the violent humans had attacked them first. Then the thought struck him. Dak could see it clearly now – one of the contingent must have said something while they flew, thinking they were safe. The humans beneath heard it and attacked because their violent little minds couldn't comprehend the idea. Priya and the others had no choice but to kill the humans who'd heard them.

Growling into the darkness, Dak found two more piles of embers further down the mountain surrounded by a multitude of boot prints and three broken trees. He sniffed at them and caught the scent of Garmod and Pantar, with a broken sword lying between them. Four burnt and broken wooden sticks lay scattered around a particularly rocky area with two more human bodies; one partially charred, the other missing an arm and a head. Several arrows embedded in tree trunks pointed away from the three dragon remains, and a fourth pile of smoldering embers. This one was further into the forest, away from the fighting than the others had been. None of the embers he'd found had Tog's or Priya's or his father's scent to them. He recognized only the remains of the other members of the contingent. He hung his head for all of them.

"Dakoon?" Dak's head jolted up. "My son!" Tusten's voice carried to Dak as loud as a roar, but his father's voice held barely a whisper.

Dak darted through the impeding underbrush toward the sound. A few lengths away, he found Tusten lying against a large boulder. His tail and left hind leg were missing, but those injuries paled next to the hole in his gut the size of his head. As his body slowly died, the pieces inside fell to the ground as embers.

"My son," Tusten repeated low. He almost smiled and let his head rest against the rock.

"Father," Dak whispered, "allow me to heal you."

"No," Tusten said firmly. He opened his eyes to look into Dak's. "Don't use your fire on me, Ido," he sighed. "Priya is missing." He swallowed as a few more embers dropped. "She flew into the trees after a faerie but she never emerged." He groaned. "The humans took Toggil. You must rescue him. You're his only hope to avoid torture."

"Don't speak, Father," Dak insisted. "Save your strength."

"I must," Tusten forced through clenched teeth. He drew a long breath through his nostrils then allowed his eyes to rest on Dak. "Ido," he whispered.

"Dromdan," Dak replied.

"Ido," his father forced out. "Of all the things I taught you, I failed you in the most important matter."

"No, Dromdan."

"You must understand," Tusten groaned. "The most important question in the world is...why?"

"'Why,' Father?"

"Yes," he nodded. "You must ask 'why' – always. There is a reason for every action. A purpose to every word. Understand why I taught you the things I did and you will understand me."

"Father, please ..." Dak clawed at the ground in angst.

"Don't grieve, Ido." Tusten rested his head again as the pile of embers underneath him grew. "I go to join your mother in the World of Souls. I'll be happy and I'll watch over you."

"Dromdan...." Dak whispered, but no reply came. His face compressed as his heart ached. Dak reached forward to wrap his claw around his father's, but the body before him consumed itself in a pile of embers before he could touch it. Dak continued his movement to clutch a clawful of the remains of his father. Tears stung his eyes, but he forced them back. With a low growl, he turned to glare into the trees in the direction the humans had gone.

———

Dak slid through the trees as silent as the night. Even without his nose to the ground he easily followed the human stench. He also caught the faint piney scent of a faerie. The scent was so subtle that it might have been an ancient trace, or the creature might recently have flown directly above him.

Shadow covered him so he knew the humans wouldn't see him until it was too late for them. Memories of human encounters usually spread through the ruck rather quickly so Dak knew they had eyesight as bad as his own. The advantages he held were his other acute senses and the most important one…surprise.

As the stink started to overwhelm him, he finally saw it. An orange glow through the trees. The humans sat huddled around three small fires as if the fires would overpower all outside danger. Stupid humans.

Dak crept closer through the cover of darkness. He could hear the humans talking, their hearts beating, their lungs breathing. He would soon stop the fracas. He watched the men from only two lengths away. Their weapons – ugly metal teeth attached to the tops of wooden poles – leaned against trees. Each human appeared to also have a sword, but only a few still wore them. A pile of unstrung bows were tied together and laid next to a log. Many of the men wore remnants of the previous battle in burn marks or torn garments. Six injured men lay on cloth mats next to the fires, but the other twenty-one sat around them, congratulating each other on their night's work. These men were begging to die.

Occasionally, they would talk of having dragon for dinner then glance over their shoulders. Once in a while, one would leave the circle and return a few minutes later. Dak tried to stare past the flames into the darkness where the men went, but his eyes couldn't focus beyond the light. So he decided to investigate with a hope. He slunk through the trees around the lively circle to the far end of the light.

Only a single dragon length away, Tog lay bound on the forest floor. Chains as thick as one claw wrapped around his jaw and the rest of his massive body had been squeezed with thick leather cords to hold his wings down. His neck was strapped tightly to a sturdy tree trunk and the trees in front of him were scorched from flame. His front and rear claws were held together with the same strong leather straps.

As Dak came upon the scene, Tog's eye closed for a moment and his shoulders dropped. Dak waited until one of the humans walked over. The man looked Tog up and down but did not look past the great gray beast.

Once the man left, Dak slipped silently through the trees. Tog's four claws were bunched absurdly together partially under him. Dak knew that with only one cord broken Tog could free himself, but he used his razor sharp talons to break most of the cords.

Tog lay perfectly still while Dak worked. He kept one eye on Dak and one on the humans. Once the cords were broken, Dak looked into his friend's eye. Tog blinked at him. Dak pointed one talon to his own ear hidden behind a spiny flap on the side of his head. He pointed to his own chest then to the far side of the clearing. Tog blinked again. Dak pointed to Tog then lifted both claws in an attack position and opened his mouth in a silent growl. Then he pointed around at all the men. Tog blinked one last time.

Having given his message, Dak returned to the other side of the unobservant humans. He settled himself just outside of their firelight's reach. He couldn't see Tog, but knew he would be on the alert. As soon as a sudden burst of laughter from the group died down, Dak gave a low growl.

Only one man turned to squint into the darkness behind him. Dak's growl grew in ferocity as he remembered his father's death. These men would suffer for it. Four men stood. Every head turned toward Dak's position. He grinned as they stared into the blackness with blind eyes.

As he loosed a final warning he added a jet of flame that lit the forest around him. The men now knew their foe, but stared helplessly at the wrong one. Behind them, Tog broke free of his bonds. He leapt into the firelight, taking a swipe with his massive front claw. He knocked down three men at once then turned to swat down three more.

As men clambered for their weapons, Dak decided not to let Tog have all the fun. He attacked the men before they could pick up their swords. Even if in their fumbling they were lucky enough to grasp a weapon, its metal clattered uselessly against his rock hard scales. With a single drag of his claw across their faces or chests, the men would collapse lifeless to the ground. Having caught the humans unaware, it was like sweeping pebbles from a path.

Tog scratched down another handful of men, one that had been wearing his sword used it to hack into Tog's fragile wing membrane. He howled, but then finished off the man in front of him and turned to face his would-be assailant. Tog slowly advanced on the trembling human, who stood only as tall as the dragon's chest. He turned his head so one protruding eye could glare coldly at his previous jailer. The man backed away from the advancing dragon perhaps deciding he should have run instead. But too late.

The man backed away until he tripped over one of his dead comrades to land on his backside in the dirt. He continued his retreat until his back struck Dak's scaly front leg. As the man's face contorted in fear, he fumbled with his hand in a brown sack tied to his belt. When he pulled it out, he opened his fist to display a dozen or more large gold coins. These he offered to the black and gray dragons standing over him.

Dak's and Tog's eyes met. Tog smirked, then lunged down at the man with his jaw agape. He clamped down on the man's head and tore it clean off.

Tog spat out the lifeless skull. "Blech!" he complained. "Human!" He grinned stupidly at Dak. "By The One, Dak! I've never been so happy for you to break the rules in all my life!" he exclaimed.

Dak smiled back at his friend. "Be wary, Tog. You're starting to see things my way."

Tog chuckled, but stopped short when they heard gurgling nearby. Another man lay against a tree with claw marks across his face and neck. Blood gushed from his neck as he made guttural noises. Both dragons moved in closer to inspect him.

"You," the man said quietly as blood drippled from his mouth. "You spoke."

"Sloppy work, Dak," Tog said, shaking his head.

"I'm sure I don't know what you mean," Dak snapped back. "This is obviously one of yours!"

"But how," the man continued to mumble, "how is it possible? You...." The man's voice began to fade. "You spoke," he murmured.

Dak took pity and decided to put the man out of his misery. "Very astute," he hummed. Then with one claw he tore the man's head from his shoulders.

When he turned back to Tog, his friend had a crazed look in his eye. "What is it?" Dak asked.

"The first kill," Tog answered. "Thrilling, isn't it?" Dak could see Tog trembling from the power.

"Indeed," Dak said simply.

"Don't you feel it too?" Tog asked.

Dak began to move around the area to count the bodies. "Not this time."

"What do you mean, 'not this time'?" Tog followed him. "This is your first major kill too."

"Actually," Dak poked at a dead human. "I killed a scorrand in the Black Forest."

"What?"

"While I was following you."

Tog stuck his head in Dak's path as he moved to count the rest of the men. "By yourself?"

"I can take care of myself, you know!" Dak reproved him.

"Alright, then!"

The two dragons examined their surroundings. "Twenty-seven accounted," Dak declared.

"I agree," Tog hemmed. After a moment, he added, "Now what?"

"Now," Dak told him, "it's your responsibility to go back to the Rock Clouds and tell Rakgar what happened here. Pantar had a mate that should be informed."

"No," Tog shook his head. "I must search for Priya. I was in her contingent. She's my responsibility."

"You should go get help," Dak argued.

"My loyalty is to her!" Tog insisted.

Dak growled low in Tog's face. "Your loyalty is to Rakgar, not Priya. She is his daughter. He is your ruler! You were assigned to her contingent under the direction of Rakgar, not Priya."

Tog exhaled slowly. "You understand these things better than anyone knows."

Dak nodded. He had studied their laws for the many extra winters he had not passed the Krusible. "If I go back to tell Rakgar what has happened, I forfeit my life." He watched his friend carefully. "I will search for Priya."

"I'll help you first," Tog said.

"No." Dak looked away from his friend. Once again they would be saying good-bye. "Your duty is to inform Rakgar. Then you can be sent with a new contingent to rescue Priya...and hunt for me as well."

Silence drowned the once raucous campsite. The two friends swam in their own feelings for a moment.

Finally, Tog spoke. "You're right. I'll go back to beg assistance. Perhaps Rakgar will be lenient with you because you rescued me."

Dak nodded, but he didn't believe it.

"Where will you start?" Tog asked.

"Back at the point of attack," Dak answered. "I'll sweep the forest until I pick up her scent."

"She dove after a faerie, down the mountainside," Tog offered. "Begin your search in that direction first."

Dak nodded again. "I will." Tog began to lope away. "Tog," Dak called to him.

"Yes?"

"Give Rakgar a message for me?" Tog turned one eye on the great black dragon so he would be able to deliver the message as a memory. "Tell him I give him my wyrd I shall see Priya gets home or die trying."

"I shall."

"Shining days, my friend."

"Clear skies, Dak," Tog answered, then smiled. "I'll probably be saving your skinny neck soon."

Dak rolled his eyes. "I think I'd rather die."

"Done!"

The two friends slapped tails like hatchlings, then Dak watched Tog race into the frozen forest.

—

Dak worked his way through the forest in the same arcing pattern in which he found the dragons' embers and his father, except this time he worked his way down the mountain from the site of attack as Tog instructed. The sun crept over his head as he scoured the forest floor. Although the warmth of the sun refreshed him slightly, the bare trees didn't give him as much cover as he would have liked. He searched long into the day when he would rather have been sleeping, as his eyelids threatened to force him into an exhausted heap on the ground.

As he searched for any trace of Priya, he considered other ways to find her if this failed. Unfortunately, every scenario included humans. He prayed to any gods listening that he might find Priya alive among the bracken of the mountain, but he knew his hunt might be in vain.

Priya had been following a faerie when she disappeared, but she followed him into the trees. There should at least be a fraction of her scent somewhere. He could climb trees and try to pick up the scent, but if she had taken to the sky again when no one was looking or when the fighting had ended, the trail would be lost.

Priya had an unusual scent for a dragon, which everyone attributed to being raised with Visi. The crazy old seer also dabbled in majik so she had many strange and marvelous ingredients for her workings in her lair. For once Dak was glad the old dame rubbed so many outlandish smells onto Priya. Her unique scent should be clear enough to find.

But instead of Priya's scent, Dak found something he didn't expect. Directly in front of his claw, the outline of a bare human footprint stood out in the snow. It could have been a faerie's footprint; faeries' and humans' bodies were much alike, except that faeries had wings and pointed ears, and a faerie's skin was translucent. They could easily be mistaken for one another with a footprint such as this, but Dak couldn't smell the breathy pine scent of a faerie. It was a human print.

He took in the ground in front of him. This time he growled. There were two sets of prints here, the bare human footprint, completely separate from the booted human prints further up, but also a faerie footprint. Dak could discern it by the pointed toes of their soft boots and the scent. The two creatures must have been waiting in hiding for Priya. Faeries were very talented at majik when they put their minds to it. They must have laid a trap for her here, then lured her away from the other dragons in order to capture her. It was the only possible explanation.

Flicking his tail in frustration, Dak examined the area. He had entered a thick copse of barbed bushes. An ideal hiding spot. He turned to peer up the mountain at the site of the dragon slaughter. His eyes were keen in the daytime. As he predicted, this spot granted a commanding view of the attack.

The bare human footprint faced the scene of slaughter up the mountain. Behind it, the footprints mixed with the pointed soft boot prints. Dak breathed in the human reek of the area while evaluating the different sets of footprints. The two creatures had stood here for a few moments together. They must have engaged each other somehow because the prints were extremely close together, and blurred in areas.

Dak stepped lightly around the sets of prints. On the other side, he followed the human prints moving down the mountain to the southeast. Each print was more than two claw lengths apart – a very long stride for a human. The human must have run away. Dak sniffed the tree branches surrounding the hiding spot. He caught the scent of the faerie on the far side, in the trees. The faerie flew in a northeast direction.

Dak grumbled again as he lay down on the ground glaring at the footprints. These creatures couldn't have captured Priya unless with majik. The faerie was the most likely to be adept in the field, but not knowing which direction it might have gone, Dak couldn't follow it in the air. His only hope would be to follow the human prints. He almost jumped up from the ground to set off.

He knew he would have to deal with more humans to solve this riddle, but he couldn't do it in the daytime. At least at night he could cloak himself in darkness. If he could find the owner of the footprints that went down the mountain, he might be able to figure out what they had done with Priya.

Before the sun reached its peak, Dak had followed the footprints to the bottom of the mountain. The human had stumbled into many trees along the way.

They had even fallen to the ground several times, as if injured or sick. He supposed the deepening cold wasn't good for it, either.

When he finally reached the bottom of the mountain, towering trees crowded together to hedge his way. Hidden on the other side of these, acres of wide, cleared space stretched out before him most unnaturally. 'Farms' he'd heard them called – with human dwellings in the distance. Humans grew plants to eat. Gross. Dragons only ate plants if they were desperate – or sick.

However, the humans couldn't grow anything in these expansions of dirt with a snowstorm coming. Dak knew he couldn't cross the fields during the day with no cover, so he crawled into the overgrown brush next to the field to wait for his opportunity.

10

Guile

Philip drummed his fingers on the arm of his throne as Murthur recited the schedule for the day, which included the ever-persistent lords. When Murthur finally stopped, Philip stilled his fingers as well. "Still no word of Bragon?" he asked without lifting his eyes. He kept his voice low in order not to alert the witnesses in the court to his anxiety. It had been three days and Philip hated waiting any longer than necessary.

"No, My Lord," Murthur answered. As he spoke the doors to the great hall swung open, so he added, "Perhaps this is the news you await."

Philip lifted his eyes anticipating a messenger from the outer villages. Hopeful young men waiting to some-day join the guards were often used as messengers between the cities and villages. But instead of a single villager, a lieutenant of the guard and a commoner entered the hall.

"Your names!" General Murzod demanded from his post beside the prince. Philip almost winced at his voice, but kept his demeanor calm. Bragon would never have spoken before the prince.

The lieutenant knelt on one knee and motioned for the commoner to do the same. Placing his fist on his chest he said, "Lieutenant Torgon, Sire. I was sent on an errand by General Bragon three days ago. It took slightly longer than requested, but I've returned with a villager from Carpan Stream Village."

The name of the village reminded Philip of the onerous lords waiting for him. "Ah, yes," he nodded. He would rather have received news of his general, but this would be nice to have done. "What is your name, sir?" he asked, looking over the head of the man.

"Sherped, Your Majesty," said the man. He wore ragged, weather-worn clothes, but a brand new coat covered most of the filth.

"Sherped," Philip repeated. "How long have you lived in Carpan Stream Village?"

"All my long sixty-two years, Sire. My family has farmed those lands for five generations and I continue that legacy."

"Very good," Philip nodded. Finally, someone he could trust to know the goings-on in the countryside. He had a good mind to engage this man more often.

"And to whom have you paid your taxes these long years, Master Sherped?"

"Taxes, Sire?"

Philip glanced briefly at Torgon's head, then back at the villager's. "You do pay your taxes, do you not?"

"Yes, Sire. Of course, Sire," the man repeated. It was, of course, punishable by imprisonment to admit otherwise.

"Carpan Stream Village lies between the lands of Lord Surcund and Lord Harcast, does it not?"

"It does, Sire."

"So, to which of these nobles does your village pay their taxes?" Philip's patience wore thin, but he held to the hope that this simple man would be honest.

Sherped's head hung.

"Do you understand the question?" Murzod barked from Philip's side. But Philip raised a hand to silence him.

"Have no fear," the lieutenant whispered to the man beside him. "The prince will deal fairly with you."

"Yes, sir," Sherped answered with his face to the floor. "I understand the question, but," he continued to hem, "I don't want to be the cause of any trouble, sir."

Philip leaned forward, staring hard at the man's balding head. "You'll be doing a great service to your crown prince by answering the question honestly," he said. "If any man should persecute you for such, I will see to his punishment personally. Now," he insisted in a gentler tone, "to whom do you pay your taxes?"

Not a soul breathed while they waited for the answer and come it did. "Both, Sire."

The law of the land was such that nobles collected taxes of thirty percent of one's income in the king's name. Then those nobles would keep the first ten percent and send the remaining twenty percent to Kingstor. Philip felt his ears burn red. "Both?" he asked, aghast.

"Yes, Sire."

"How is this possible?"

"When tax time comes around at harvest, sir, we's gather thirty percent of our wares for Surcund and thirty percent for Harcast."

"Do you mean to tell me you're paying sixty percent of the value of your harvest to these men?"

"Yes, Sire." Sherped kept his nose to the floor the entire time he spoke.

"How long have you done this?" Philip asked, hoping this was a fresh complication.

"Most of my life, Sire."

Philip silently struggled to keep his teeth from grinding. "Why would they do this?" Philip asked no one in particular but everyone in the room. A few nobles present averted their eyes as he searched them.

"Sire," Torgon spoke up. "I've heard of this deceit before." Before continuing, Philip thought he saw the faint movement of his lieutenant's head in the direction of Murzod, but he stood up to finish. "Nobles who own land on either side of a village both tax the villagers. For the most part they leave the villagers alone, as long as they keep up on their taxes; and they split the profit equally. It's always done with consent from both parties of nobles."

"Then why would they complain about it now?" Philip asked him.

Again, Torgon's eyebrows gave the distinct sign of a glance toward Murzod. When he saw it the second time, Philip realized the reason. Murzod came from a family of nobles; most of the officers of the guard did. They were the only ones wealthy enough to afford the tribute fee in order to test for ascension. Philip wondered if this crime perpetuated more than these men admitted. "If the nobles have some other dispute, they might use this as leverage, Sire."

"Sherped," Philip said to the man. Seeing his shoulders jolt from his name being called again, Philip thought he might know more. "You know, don't you? You know what this argument stems from." It wasn't a question and Philip would demand an answer. Whether now or in private.

"Rumor, Sire." Sherped shrugged. "Just rumor."

"What is the rumor, then?" Philip was losing control over his anger. He wanted this solved.

"Surcund," the man hesitated slightly, "he has a daughter, Sire." With these words, Philip could imagine the rest of the story. "Harcast has never been married and she is a beauty, Sire..."

"This is madness!" Philip interrupted. "I'll have their heads!" he raged. "Murthur!"

"Yes, Sire."

Philip lowered his eyes to focus on Sherped's. His brow was withered with sun and age, but the moment his eyes met the prince's, Philip could see wisdom and kindness in them that could only come from a life of honest, hard work. "Take this down," he indicated to Murthur. "Surcund and Harcast are to return fifty years of back taxes to the villagers. I strip them of their rank and lands. Sherped" – at this the villager's head snapped up – "and whomever he deems worthy of the position are to take up the two lordships in their steads. I trust they'll run a more equitable community than those two demons! Surcund and Harcast will be cast into prison for ten years each."

"Sire," Murzod nearly shouted, "Isn't that going a bit too far?"

But Philip stood to stare into the face of his general. "And if I should receive word of any other nobles levying the same injustice, their restitution will be the same. Let a decree go forth as such." Murzod swallowed, but said nothing. "General Murzod, assign a guard to accompany this man back to his village to gather his belongings. In a month's time Sherped will return here to claim his lordship. Have two more guards arrest the scum Harcast and Surcund."

"Yes, My Lord."

After much bowing and thanking, the general and the new lord left the audience hall. Philip collapsed in his throne. These vultures were the very types of nobles Bragon had warned him against. Philip's eyes habitually moved to his right to search out Bragon. He wondered if his mentor would agree with his actions. He longed for the approval of at least one of the two men in his life whose opinions mattered to him. But the vacancies where both of them should be only reminded him of more pressing matters.

"No word from General Bragon, Sire?" Torgon asked. Philip shook his head. "Give me leave to seek him out, Sire, and I'll bring word."

Philip looked up at the lieutenant's forehead. The man seemed to know his mind; perhaps it would be best to send him. "A better idea was never spoken. Go with haste."

II

Odor and Tracks

A gentle snow fell during the day. It wasn't much, but it was enough to cover the footprints in the dirt. Dak wasn't bothered, though. He knew he wouldn't be able to see the footprints at night, anyway, but he could follow the owner's scent. The snow might have swallowed any traces of the scent for another dragon, but not Dak. Although much sweeter than that of the humans he and Tog had killed, this scent contained the same metallic flavor, but milder, or diluted somehow. He wouldn't easily forget it. He would sniff every human within a day's flight if he must.

After another restless day's sleep – in which he dreamt of scorrands that smelled of humans chasing him through the mountains – Dak woke when the moons had already risen. He hadn't rested well, but fire burned hot in his belly, making him eager to continue his quest.

He soon picked up the human scent where he had left it, at the edge of the now-frosted forest. He followed the human's trail along the edge of the wide spaces for a ways before it met a small dry stream bed that branched from the mountain. A rickety wooden bridge crossed over the stream bed, but he avoided it. With his breath melting the snow as he moved, he followed the scent until it crossed the stream bed and seemed to change. The human scent grew strong on the opposite bank. With the meager light of the moons, Dak could only surmise the owner of the footprints might have collapsed on the edge of the stream bed. Then a second human scent mingled with the first. It smelled strongly of plants, dirt and human sweat. After melting the snow away, Dak could barely make out a second set of footprints. These were larger and clad with heavy boots, similar to those the men at the dragon slaughter had worn.

Dak endeavored to interpret the signs he saw on the ground along with the scents. The barefoot human had toppled next to the stream bed. The shod human had approached the first then left again, but impressionably under a great weight – the boot prints leaving the site were deeper than the ones that arrived. As the shod human staggered back the way he had come, the first scent became vague. The second human must have carried the first away! And there was no mistaking their direction.

———

Dak followed the second scent quietly. It wasn't hard. The stink oozed from the ground on which he walked. He knew he would have to take great care approaching any humans. They might not smell or even hear him coming, but he could see only as well as they could at night, so sneaking up might be difficult.

The scent travelled an almost precisely straight line through the fields. The boot steps strayed only occasionally when encountering a large rock or something else in the path, so Dak assumed they moved with haste. Dak, however, slithered through the fields keeping his body close to the ground and his eyes ever-watchful around him. He carried a curse in his heart. He knew the first human he had trailed down the mountain had contributed in some way to the attack on the dragons and the disappearance of Priya. He held the second human at fault by association with the first.

Before long, Dak saw flickering lights ahead. Taking a chance, he spread his wings to lift himself from the ground leaving his tracks behind then he tip-taloned toward a wooden building large enough to accommodate a handful of dragons comfortably. Next to it, a round, metal building towered at least twice its height, but only a quarter of the size around. Another smaller building with many windows nestled amid some oaks on the other side. A ghost of smoke rose from the smaller building and light flickered in two windows, indicating inhabitants.

As he neared the habitations, Dak was assailed by the fetid odor of smoke, humans and dirt. The closer he got, the more the stench of mammal filth threatened his sanity. As he crept closer, fire bubbled up in his throat, but he choked it back down. If he vomited fire now, the chase would end too soon.

When he got outside the largest of the buildings, he heard animals inside. Some dogs were locked inside, but they could sense the danger through the feeble wooden wall. The barks grew louder as Dak approached from the rear. He couldn't hear anything for the noise and was tempted to knock down the walls to silence the fiends. But instead slipped around the side.

A group of more large oak trees mixed with tall pines stood away from the wooden building. Enshrouded under the blanket of snow, they offered Dak an adequate hiding place. He silently made his way to their shadows in a couple of stealthy bounds. As he settled into the cover, a hatch swung free from the back of the little dwelling with the flickering lights. A human man stood in the moonlight for a moment and Dak froze, hoping he blended with the nighttime.

"Quiet there!" the man yelled at the beasts barking in the night.

"What is it, Jarek?" Dak heard a woman's voice issue from inside.

"All's well, Boorda," the man, Jarek, answered. "Probably just a mouse or something in the barn."

With the barking silenced, Dak could better hear the humans speak. As Jarek went back in, Dak closed his eyes to listen closely.

"I don't like it, Jarek," Boorda whispered. "What will we do with her?"

"We're Hamees. We've made oaths to care for anyone in need." Dak had to strain to hear Jarek's answer. "We'll do as our oaths decree, but for now, we'll go to sleep." The voices ceased and the little lights inside guttered.

Dak crouched in his hiding place debating his next move. He assumed this human had something to do with the attack on the dragons and/or the disappearance of Priya. But what if he was wrong? What if Priya had simply flown off somewhere else altogether? What if she left with the faerie, whether willingly or not? The faeries had always been allies of the dragons. Dak knew he couldn't assume them to be anything in these circumstances. Perhaps Priya had escaped with assistance from the faerie and was at this moment safe with them. He prayed to the gods that he had misconjectured and Priya was far away with the faeries.

Dak brooded. He assumed one of two things had happened to Priya: either she was safe with the faeries, or she had been captured by the humans. He found it absurd that any human might capture a dragon, but then, it had happened to Tog even with his obvious advantages. Perhaps the faerie had made Priya invisible so she could fly away with him unnoticed. But if that was the case, then why wouldn't she have let the others know? Why wouldn't she have rescued Tog herself? Dak's mind spun. Maybe she had gone for reinforcements. Maybe she thought the others were all dead. She might be lamenting their loss now while the faeries attended her.

Even if all that were true, the question remained, why had the human whose footsteps he followed down the mountain watched the dragon slaughter from afar? Why would they run away, down the mountain, and collapse in a field? Had they been running away or toward? The human's sweet-smelling scent was fresh. The timing of its actions fit what had happened to his friends up the mountain.

But he was here now. His friends were dead. One of these humans had seen everything. The other assisted the first. He must learn more. Once he decided to stay and observe the humans, his mind rested. But he knew he couldn't remain so close to their habitations.

Dak allowed a whisper of a winter breeze to waft him back into the snow-covered fields. He floated far enough over them that his tracks wouldn't be seen – at least not right away. He would give himself a couple of sun cycles to ascertain what he could. It wouldn't be pleasant work, to be sure. The smell alone might be fatal! But it was his duty to find out whatever he could. Then he might have something to report when Tog returned with others.

Luckily, clumps of large trees interspersed among the humans' fields. Dak found one such abbreviated forest for slumber. The trees would be tall enough for him to climb to watch the humans, and they were thick enough for him to hide from them.

Dak had a punctuated rest while wrestling with so many questions. Before the sun peeked over the horizon, the humans began to stir. For the first time in his life, Dak would see how humans lived. He tried to callous himself against the many atrocities he might be forced to witness.

He was awake when Jarek emerged from his little wooden building before any light filled the sky. At least he assumed it was Jarek. The human was wrapped in so many furs and thick leathers that Dak couldn't see much of the human underneath. The walking ball of clothing plodded out to the larger wooden building he had called a "barn". He stayed there until the sun rose, then he came out with a bucket in each hand. He took those into the dwelling.

The sun unveiled to Dak many other buildings which he had not perceived in the night, all similar to Jarek's. Several other barns and buildings clustered together, with many smaller dwellings among them. Behind one, a mass of cattle slept. Behind another, flocks of small, feathered creatures scratched at the ground. A human village.

Humans began to flow in and out of all the buildings as the sun climbed in the sky. Watching the village activity, Dak pondered its resemblance to a living, breathing animal. This animal was strong. These humans were capable of wondrous feats. Perhaps even concealing a dragon.

Dak's hiding place was close enough to see the humans' comings and goings, but not close enough to hear them speak or see the details of their work. He held his breath when Jarek came out of his dwelling and headed for the trees where Dak had hidden himself during the night. But before he reached it, Jarek moved backward along the same track Dak had taken around the area and barn. Suddenly, the man ran deep into the village, only to return with half a dozen more humans. Dak had heard the saying, "humans reproduce as fast as a cloud makes raindrops", but he hadn't believed it until now.

The group of men with Jarek milled about the area where Dak had first crouched behind the barn. Some of them wandered a few steps away to stare out over the icy fields beyond. Dak froze whenever their faces seemed to turn toward the grove where he hid. Eventually, he exhaled when the humans dispersed.

Later in the day, Dak awoke when Jarek rode out of the barn astride a brown horse. The two creatures meandered through the fields in the general direction of Dak's covert. As they approached the spot where Dak's tracks told the tale of his landing and running into these very trees, his breath stopped again.

"Ho, Jarek!" a man's voice echoed across the fields from the other direction. Dak let only his eyes swivel to see another human man, covered in furs, sitting atop a brown and white horse.

Another step of Jarek's beast and Dak's tracks would have been blatant, but Jarek turned to face the caller. "Ho, Rika!" he hailed.

The two men rode their mounts to meet each other in front of the very coppice where Dak nested over their heads. "I heard you had a visitor last night." Rika had a deep, throbbing voice.

Jarek nodded. "Seems so."

"Dragons don't come into this area much." Dak's heart pounded at Rika's words. "We'll set up a watch for the night."

"Boorda would appreciate that," Jarek said.

"Do you think it has anything to do with the woman you found by the stream?" Rika asked.

"No way to know." Jarek scratched his forehead under his hat. "But it's all very unsettling. Boorda can sense it the most."

"Would you like me to shelter the woman for you?"

"Thank you," Jarek said. "But that isn't necessary. She has recovered and will be leaving soon."

"Very well." Rika turned his horse around. "I'll see you tonight."

"Thank you!" Jarek called after the man as he galloped his horse into his fields. With one last long glance into the trees and the field around him, Jarek reined in his horse and turned toward his home.

With a sigh, Dak knew he wouldn't be going anywhere this night.

—

"Yes, Sire." The old man in front of Philip scratched his white hair then adjusted the several amulets on the front of his robes. "I got your message about the faeries' information."

Philip tapped his finger on the desk. "You look ten years older than you did three months ago, Travaith."

"Long days and much longer nights will age a man, no matter what youth spells he knows," Travaith said, rubbing his chin.

"You've been working with my father's physician?"

"Day and night."

Philip sighed. "I know I've come to you too often recently, but the faeries make my skin crawl. I need to know if I can trust them."

"They make me anxious as well, My Lord, but..." His voice trailed off into an incoherent rasp.

Philip stood from his chair behind his desk. Stepping to the majishun's side, he placed a hand on his shoulder as a teardrop traced a wrinkle in the old man's cheek. "I know I've been relying on you a lot lately. Perhaps I should consult someone who – "

"No, My Lord!" Before he could finish, the white-haired head jerked up to stare in Philip's eyes with the icy blue gaze he knew so well. "Please, I'm doing the best I can!"

"You misunderstand," Philip insisted. "I don't mean to replace you. Your service has been invaluable to our family these many years. I would never dare to insult your loyalty!"

"No," Travaith shook his head. "Perhaps it would be better if you consulted another majishun. I could never save a queen for your father. I'm unsure I can save your father now." He hung his head.

"Travaith, who else could I possibly turn to?" Philip stepped to the window overlooking the frozen king's forest. "No one on the Majikal Guild is as experienced as you. I would be forced to appoint a faerie as the court majishun, and I am not prepared to do that." At this, Travaith looked out from under reddened eyelids. Having his attention, Philip stared at him. "I have no one else I can trust right now."

The majishun covered his face in his hands. "I've seen the dragons leave the Rock Clouds, but I haven't been able to replicate any of the other things the faeries have seen in their crystal ball. It's hard enough to replicate answers to my own questions, let alone answers to questions I can't begin to understand. It could be the way they ask their questions in the Faerie tongue might make the difference, but, again, I can only guess."

"So what does this mean?" Philip asked as he turned back to the window.

"I'm not sure." Travaith cleared his throat. "The only advice I can give you is this." He took a deep breath as Philip turned to face his trusted majishun again. "You must decide for yourself if you should trust them or not. As for me, I will continue to hunt down any answers I can. Until the day I die."

12

Night Watchers

As night crawled on, the human men took turns staring into the darkness. Dak could just see the outlines of at least two men at all times, when they moved to change positions or trade places, which they did often. Through the vigil he kept strictly to the trees, only alighting in the tangled bushes below to rest occasionally. No matter how many times he moved back and forth, the humans never seemed to notice him.

While watching the men in their diligence, he wondered about their purpose. To give an alarm about dragons in the area was obvious enough. But why? Humans didn't care enough to protect each other, so why would they do it? Were the homes and barns communal property?

Yes, he decided, that must be it. They must be extremely territorial creatures. So possessive of their goods they insist everyone in the community protect everything. Useful information should he ever return to any rucks.

The next day Dak observed the humans going about their business. No one bothered about his tracks again. In fact, Boorda took some sort of tool to the ground to obliterate them. The only incident happened as the sun slid down in the sky; Jarek happened upon Dak's prints in the field and followed them to the trees. Dak crouched under a fallen log and watched.

Normally, Dak would pounce before his prey realized what was happening, but having seen how quickly the humans could multiply, he withheld to see what the man might do. Jarek peered into the darkness from the edge of the trees, but never actually entered them to investigate further. Thus saving his own life.

As night fell again Dak's thoughts turned to Tog. He must have reached the Rock Clouds by now. Hopefully he would return with a fresh dragon contingent within three sun cycles. He had until then to gather any information on Priya's whereabouts then decide what to do with himself.

Since only one human slept outside of Jarek's house, he couldn't go wandering about or flying around their dwellings, so Dak decided to go back to the mountain, to the site of the dragon slaughter. On silent wings, Dak glid over the fields so low he could have dragged his claws in the snow. He made sure to keep his wooded hiding spot between himself and the human on watch. Just in case.

He spent most of the night circling the battle site with his nose to the ground. He trooped through the forest or flew over the branches. He went back down the mountain and repeated his search of the area where he had found the barefoot human and faerie footprints. He toiled the entire night, but came away with no more enlightenment than when he had left the mountain the first time.

Dak returned to his wooded hiding place with his fire roiling deep inside him. He longed to uproot the trees around him and then do the same to all the human buildings. Perhaps if he burned everything down Priya would be exposed. But he knew he couldn't act in any purposeful way the humans might interpret as intelligence or even anger. The very fact he had prowled around a human home but left it untouched might be seen by some dragons as a violation of all they strove to conceal. He knew he must be more careful not to leave traces of his presence. But he also knew if he stayed in his thatched cage another night he would never solve this riddle.

Finally, the following night presented a clear way to Dak. The humans must have thought the danger abated, for they all stayed in their flammable little dwellings in the darkness. Not only had the humans seemingly given up their possessive behavior, but the three moons in Avonoa's sky gave off only a sliver of light.

When the moons hovered overhead, Dak slipped out of the trees. He kept to his original tracks to gain access to the barren fields. He held still for a moment with his eyes closed to listen for any movement or recognition from the humans. The only sound he heard was the wind chilling the snow-covered ground.

Dak used the wind to fill his wings. He swept his wings a few times to hover over the field. Then he paused again and listened – still nothing but the wind wrapping its icy fingers around his limbs.

Dak pressed his wings harder to lift into the air. He opened his eyes but detected no movement from the little group of buildings. A wayward cloud covered half of the middle moon, lending a slight addition of darkness. So Dak set off over the human dwellings as silent as the brittle cold he cut through.

The village sat not far from the protection of the mountains. From the air, Dak could see the buildings clustered like square logs floating together on a sea of white. Large, open fields encircled the village, broken only by occasional groves of trees. Within the circle of fields were numerous farms enclosed by hedges of stone, wood or wire. Different kinds of animals crowded inside the hedged areas. Some were small and round, others feathered, still more large and hairy. Dak recognized horses and pigs, but couldn't name any others. Many more trees dappled the area around the pens then reached into the village as well.

Dak could make out the shingled rooftops of the human homes along with smaller rooftops thatched with straw or large Bluebrush needles. All these little buildings and homes huddled together in a circle like stones around a fire pit. A clear track, wide enough for a dragon to march along, wrapped through the little village, passed each building and circled around the few dozen buildings in the middle. Then the path wove its way back the way it came, between the trees to the mountains beyond, forming a natural pass.

Of all the inner buildings in the village, one stood out in stark contrast to the humble structures around it. Dak wondered as to the use of this edifice. It was much larger than all the other buildings. Small windows dotted the plainer structures, but this one had two large windows, one on the front and one on the back, stretching the height of the building from roof to ground. It had one path around the outside and one leading away in the front, both paths had been lovingly removed of all traces of snow. Even the larger track through the village still had blotches of ice on it, but this building didn't have a speck of snow on the trail around it and not a single footprint led off the trail.

As he circled over this structure he came into a better view of the front. He immediately dropped his wings, attempting to dive into the cover of the trees. But when he looked back, the humans he thought had seen him hadn't moved. They still stood on either side of the large window with their faces and hands turned to the sky. Changing his course again, he flew a little closer to see that the things he thought were humans were actually their images scratched out of tree trunks.

On the structure itself, intricate designs were painted on the two doors at either side of the large windows, and delicate scrollwork covered the eaves around the building. None of the other buildings had such decorations, so Dak knew the building must mean something to the humans. After careful inspection, he decided to avoid it entirely. The motionless humans in front of the building gave him the strangest feeling, especially because they stared straight up at him.

Perhaps a different vantage will give some direction, Dak thought to himself.

He found a spot closer to the humans, along the wide track leading to and from the village but thick enough with trees and shrubbery to hide him. He saw no sign that Priya, or any dragon other than himself, had ever been anywhere near these humans. Unless they had hidden her in the barn – and he was sure he would have heard the humans discuss that – she must have left the mountain with the faerie. However, he had no proof of either scenario, and no more clues to follow.

13

Somber Tidings

The door closed silently behind Philip. He stood in the middle of the hall for a moment, aware of being watched, but not caring. He had just come from his father's bedside. King Paudie was frail and weak, much more than any man at the young age of fifty should be. Physicians could do nothing. Faerie shamans could do nothing. He hadn't eaten for days although his personal servant tried several times a day. This last visit had been the worst by far, his father not noticing Philip for who he was or even knowing he was there for most of the day. Philip closed his eyes.

He will be gone soon. I must accept this, Philip thought. I will be king.

The thought of losing his father and becoming king in the same moment weakened his knees, but he stood firm. When the threat of moisture had been pulled away from his lashes, yet again, he opened them. He would mourn when no one else could see.

He had stayed in his father's chamber far too long hoping to see a light of recognition in his eyes. The day wore on. Philip eventually had to force himself to leave. Somehow he knew those moments would be the last.

The pounding of boots against the floor brought him back from his grief. "Sire!" General Murzod hailed him. After a brief salute, he said quickly, "Lieutenant Torgon has returned."

Philip tore past the general. "It's only been one day. He must have never stopped to rest!"

"He's waiting in the audience hall, Sire."

"Did he say anything?"

Murzod practically ran to keep up. "No, Sire. He would report only to you."

As much as he longed to know the tidings, he couldn't help but admire the lieutenant's loyalty. Certainly a man worth having at my side, Philip thought. Perhaps I should promote him to captain for his efficiency.

Philip burst through the doors of the audience hall, not even waiting for the guards to open them for him. Torgon fell to one knee when his prince entered. "Lieutenant Torgon," Philip said, looking over his head. "What news?"

Torgon stood but turned his face to the ground. "I'm afraid I bring ill tidings, Sire."

"General Bragon?"

After a moment's pause, "He's dead, Sire."

The weakness returned to Philip's knees. "Dead?"

As Philip tottered past him toward his throne, Torgon continued. "I know you were close to him, Sire, so I've told no one else."

"Thank you, Lieutenant," Philip said as he gingerly sat on his throne. "And the rest of the men?"

"All dead, Sire." Torgon's voice was no more than a whisper.

"All?" Philip asked the floor.

"I came upon the slaughter part-way up the mountain of Golthoth," Torgon answered. "It seems they had captured a dragon, but he escaped somehow. Thus they no longer had the element of surprise that they used to their advantage when they first attacked." Torgon paused again. "I sent men from the nearest village to gather the bodies."

Philip once again took note that this man seemed to know his prince's mind in these matters. "Thank you again, Lieutenant." He took a deep breath and clenched his fist. "The faeries were supposed to be there to prevent something like this. Did you find their bodies among the dead?"

Torgon shook his head again. Raising it back to the prince he said, "I stopped at their rooms in the village on the way back to the castle."

"Were they there?"

"Only one, Sire. I told him to follow me with haste."

"And I came as soon as I could, Sire." Kradik's voice floated into the room with him as silent as a shadow.

"Where were you when this tragedy occurred?" Philip asked through grit teeth.

"When I left Bragon's side, we had been successful with the dragons. We had killed all but one whom we took captive."

"What? Killed all?"

"It was necessary, My Lord." Kradik stood before him with his hands together. "I sent my apprentice to relay a message to the Faerie Council about our activities and I returned to our rooms in the village with Bragon's permission."

"He gave you leave?"

"Yes, Sire." Kradik stepped closer. "I cannot watch the future of every creature at every moment. Certainly not without my equipment. If I had known, I would have warned Bragon. I'm sorry for your loss, Sire."

Philip didn't return the incline of the faerie's head. His instinct told him the faeries knew this would happen and adeptly avoided being involved in it. But he had no way to prove it. "Alright." He pinched his nose between his eyes as he thought of what to do next. "Kradik, thank you for your assistance. You are dismissed."

"I'll notify Your Highness immediately if any more threats from the dragons are forthcoming." Kradik bowed deeply and left the audience hall.

"Sire," Murzod said once he had left. "You must choose a new Royal General immediately."

Philip took a breath, but before he could respond Torgon burst out, "Give him time to grieve before you press for a promotion, Murzod!"

Philip saw red rise in Murzod's head like wine in a goblet so he lifted a hand to silence them both. They were both in the right, although Philip had to agree with Torgon that Murzod's request was untimely. Philip swallowed his grief. "You're right, Murzod." Then he turned to Torgon. "Bragon trusted you, didn't he?" Philip assumed he had, since Bragon had chosen Torgon for a delicate errand earlier.

"I believe so, Sire," he answered. "Fathers have a tendency to trust their sons."

Philip blinked in surprise and dropped his eyes from the man's hair to his eyes. He felt as if he looked into Bragon's face again, but this man was young, perhaps only twenty. "Bragon was your father?"

"Yes, Sire."

Fond memories of horse racing and tree climbing with another young man tickled Philip's mind. He remembered Bragon speaking of his eldest son, but Philip hadn't seen him in years. Philip thought of the loyalty Torgon had shown in bringing this tragic news straight to him. He thought of his own poor father, the king, lying sick in his bed. If his father had suffered such a horrific death as Bragon had, would he have been able to think clearly enough to complete such an important duty?

"You saw your father's mangled body and you returned here, amidst your own grief, to bring tidings of a dear friend to your prince?"

Torgon simply nodded.

"Such faithfulness I have never seen." Philip stepped down from his throne to place his hand on the young man's shoulder. "He was like a father to me as well." Torgon tried to look into the prince's eyes, but his own filled with tears. "Go," Philip said. "Go to your mother and grieve with her. When you're sufficiently recovered, return to my side to take your father's place as Royal General."

"What?!" Murzod shouted.

"Yes, Sire." Torgon never even lifted his eyes at the news. When Philip removed his hand, Torgon saluted him again, then left the chamber filled with sorrow.

"That ungrateful troll," Murzod said. "He never even said 'thank you'."

Philip turned away from the double doors to look at Murzod. "Should one ever be grateful for being burdened with more responsibility?"

"It is a fabulous promotion for one so young."

"I am young."

Murzod inspected the floor. "I don't believe he is as deserving as you, My Lord."

"And my judgment means nothing?" Philip's temper rose in the silence. "Murzod," Philip said allowing his eyes to drift up to the man's hairline. "For your slander of a superior, I think you should take the lieutenant's place until such time as you come to recognize the true definition of rank."

"But Sire – "

Philip pointed at the double doors. "Go."

In his grief, Philip had allowed himself to make an enemy of a lieutenant and a friend of a general. But to have Torgon by his side instead of Murzod, he knew it would be worth it

14

Passing Ways

"I'm a dragon!" A small human squeal tore Dak from his slumber. He had nestled under some bushes in the night only to find them a thorny haven. But as bothersome as it was, he knew no humans would venture near.

Dak barely opened his eyelids as the little creature – wearing breeches like the men and possibly even more outer clothing – jumped around in the snow near his hiding place. "Come back, Harry!" another small human called after him. "Mother said not to play near the forest!" This human had visible long, dark curls falling down her back from under a thick cap. She wore the flowing skirt like a human woman, but she was much smaller. She didn't wear as much covering, but she also didn't seem as inclined to roll in the cold, wet snow.

Human children, Dak thought. Poor, doomed souls.

"A dragon wouldn't hurt another dragon, Tara!" Little Harry danced closer to the trees.

"I'm telling Mother!" Tara disappeared into one of the little dwellings.

Harry skipped over the frosty ground then jumped over a log. He flapped his arms in the air with his face scrunched together. Dak had to suppress a laugh, as he was certain he must have worn the same look on his face the first time he attempted flight. He found himself almost hoping the boy would find the ability within himself and fly away. But instead, the boy ducked through the trees in Dak's direction. He stomped on the ground with both feet. Baring what Dak could only assume were tiny splayed fingers under their covers, he made a fierce face, but looked more like he'd caught a particularly nasty bone between his teeth. "Rahhh!" he yelled, but his roar stopped short.

The little boy dropped all pretenses to squint into the darkness in front of him. Dak stared back at the fearless little human. For a moment, their eyes locked. The fake dragon stood with a gaping mouth as Dak winked one eye.

"Harrison!" screamed a woman's voice from the edge of the forest. After recovering himself from his mother's abrupt appearance, Harry whirled around to face the woman who stood with her fists on her hips.

"Mother!" he called. He lifted a shaky finger in Dak's direction, but his words were cut off.

"Get back here this instant!" yelled the menacing mother. Even with her slight build Dak admitted he might have been terrified if she'd yelled at him like that.

"But…" Harry started as he tumbled through the trees toward her.

"Not a word, young man!" the woman shook a finger in his direction.

"But, Mother…" He finally reached the woman who attacked one of his ears.

"You are not to go near the forest!" she continued her tirade as she coerced the boy, screaming in pain, back into their home. Dak's brow creased in worry. These humans were everything he had been told – ruthless, unrelenting and cruel, even to their own young. Imagine what they might do to the likes of him. He must leave tonight and never return.

Dak watched with sorrow as he thought of the little boy. What evil punishment might he be enduring right now? He had made up his mind to burst from his hiding place this very evening and save the child from torture when the front entrance to Jarek's dwelling in the distance changed his mind.

A large wooden box on wheels attached to Jarek's brown horse waited in front of the structure. Small boxes and bags filled the majority of it. Out of the little building came Jarek and two women. One woman had short brown hair and wore a faded green dress with a thin cloth around her shoulders. She nodded her head to the other woman, saying something Dak couldn't hear over the stamping of the horse.

The other woman towered over the first, almost as tall as the man, Jarek. She wore a light blue dress showing more of her ankles than the other village women Dak had seen. From this distance he immediately assumed it was the same woman who had spoken to him in the Black Forest. The long golden curls cascading down her back certainly screamed of some relationship between the two. In the clear daylight, Dak could make out the same tilted, almond eyes and high cheekbones as the woman from the World of Souls. But this woman had substance. When she stepped on the ground, he heard the click of her heel. When she walked next to the horse, it acknowledged her presence with a toss of its head. The woman from the World of Souls and the woman in front of Dak now had the same oval face and the same full lips. They could almost be the same person except for the eyes. The woman in front of him turned to look into the forest in his direction. Instead of the beautiful summer-sky blue eyes he had seen in the Black Forest, this woman's eyes were a brilliant emerald-green color.

Jarek helped the taller woman up to sit on the edge of the box directly behind the horse. He bent briefly toward the woman on the ground, then climbed up to sit next to the yellow-haired woman, who had thrown a thick blanket around her shoulders. He took up some thin straps that were attached to the horse.

After shouting a command, the horse pulled the rolling box and its occupants away.

The box clattered past the buildings on the wide path toward Dak. Silently he watched as it passed under the trees in front of him, snaking its way to the mountain pass. As it rattled by, the breeze carried the smallest hint of its occupants. There could be no mistake. The golden-haired woman leaving with Jarek was the barefoot human Dak had been chasing.

15

Elucidation

Prince Philip sat behind an ornate writing desk in an office adjacent to the audience hall. Today he was overseeing preparations for his father's funeral and his own eventual coronation. Until yesterday he hadn't been able to accept that his father would die, but after the news of Bragon and sending Torgon off to make similar arrangements for his own father, he decided it was time. Murthur sat opposite him, helping him row through the harder decisions. Philip would never admit it, but having Murthur as a constant in his life had helped him in more ways than he knew.

Suddenly an urgent knock came at the door. "Enter," Philip said.

A lieutenant whose name Philip didn't know came through the doors. "I'm sorry to interrupt, My Lord," the man said, kneeling and saluting, "but a woman has arrived who demands to see the king."

"No one sees the king," Philip said, hardly lifting his eyes. "Tell her to go away."

"But she insists, My Lord," he said again. "She is berating my men."

"Lieutenant," Philip put his pen down, "this has happened before, hasn't it?"

"Yes, My Lord, but – " the man paused.

"But what?"

"This woman is different."

"Different how?" Philip asked with piqued interest.

"She acts like nobility, Sire. And – "

"And what?"

"She..."

"Speak your mind, Lieutenant," Philip urged.

The man held himself up straighter. "She very much resembles the fair Queen Annette."

Philip stood. "How is that possible?" he whispered.

"I don't know, Sire. But I believe her to be in earnest," the lieutenant mumbled to the floor.

"Show her into the audience hall."

"Yes, Sire," the man said quickly before he retreated.

"We'll finish this later," Philip said to Murthur.

"Yes, Sire," he answered, already tidying the papers on the desk. "Most of the arrangements are made."

Philip stepped into the audience hall to wait for the woman, but he had barely taken his throne before the doors opened again. She must have been very insistent. Indeed, he realized, she must have been waiting just outside the doors. Only with a noble's attitude could a visitor gain access in this manner.

When she strode into the room, one step ahead of the guard, Philip could immediately see what the man had described. Although she wore a commoner's dress, which was too short at the ankle and wrist, she held her head high. She walked with a straight back, gliding on her feet. Philip could see his father's almond-shaped eyes, in fact, his own eyes, in hers. However, they weren't the same muted greenish-blue; they were a shocking shade of green. He had never seen anything like it – they were the shade of sparkling emeralds. They looked almost inhuman.

But otherwise the woman looked nothing like Philip. On the walls around them were four life-size portraits. Philip's and his father's portraits were behind their thrones, and behind the third throne was his own dear mother's portrait. Queen Linea, the second wife of King Paudie. On the wall adjacent to the thrones the portrait of Queen Annette hung alone. King Paudie placed it there in remembrance of his first wife, the woman who carried his first child. She had been killed by a dragon in the King's Forest before the child was born – at least, that is what everyone had believed.

The woman locked eyes with Philip. He didn't even think about not looking directly into her eyes; that was the air she produced. Much the same way he had been taught. Before he could say a word, she spoke. "My name is Anna, daughter of King Paudie and Queen Annette. I demand to see my father at once."

"The king is ill. No one sees him except myself and the physicians."

"I will see him."

"What gives you the right – ?" he started.

"SHE – " she yelled, stabbing a finger at the portrait of Queen Annette on the wall. She had never even glanced at it upon entering "GIVES ME THE RIGHT!"

Philip reluctantly looked at the first queen's portrait. He didn't want to be made a fool of by a commoner, but neither did he want to refuse this woman courtesy. She did, indeed, carry herself and act like a noble.

As he inspected the portrait and the woman in turn, he could see the same delicate features in their faces. The same high cheekbones. The same curvature of their full lips. The same oval face. The same slenderness in build. The same golden hair falling in twisted locks over their shoulders and back. There was no mistaking the two women were nearly identical in appearance except for the difference in the color of their eyes. The sparking blue of Queen Annette's eyes looking at him from the wall, and the brilliant startling green eyes of the woman standing before him. She stood nearly as tall as Philip, which could be attributed to their father's height. Philip himself was exceptionally tall for a man of sixteen. He could not deny her to be his half-sister.

He stood to look at her. "Only one person can tell us the truth of it. Come with me."

The two left the audience chamber together and walked side-by-side down the corridor. They turned down another, then another, deeper into the castle. Every servant they passed gasped as they walked by. One woman even dropped her basket with a small yelp. Anna never flinched at the responses. Finally they reached the king's chamber doors, flanked by staff-guards. One of the guards opened the doors and Philip entered first.

He entered the room quietly, wondering to himself what he was doing. Should he be bothering the king with such a trivial matter, particularly if the woman wasn't who she claimed she was? His father turned to look at him when he entered. He had not done that in a long time.

"Father," Philip announced himself. "I'm sorry to bother you."

"Your visits never bother me, my son." Paudie lifted a withered hand.

"There's someone that needs to see you," Philip said. He stepped aside to reveal the golden-haired woman behind him. He hoped she would see how frail the king was and drop any pretenses. He hoped the sight of a dying man would appeal to her better judgment than to torture him more. But when she stepped forward, the king pulled his head from the pillow.

"Annette?" he whispered. "My dear, sweet Annette?"

"My name," she answered, "is Anna. I am Annette's daughter – " she paused to glance at Philip "and yours."

"Anna?" the king whispered to her, his eyes opening wide. He lifted both hands to her. "Anna, my beautiful daughter." He squeezed her hands as she sat next to him on the bed. "How is this possible?"

"Yes," Philip muttered, joining them at the head of his father's bed. "I'd like to know that, too."

"My mother bore me before the gray dragon killed her," Anna told the king. "I was raised by an old woman, far up in the mountains."

She opened her mouth to continue, but the king shook his head. "Nothing else matters. You've returned to us." He let go of one of her hands and reached it out to Philip. "Philip," he said, taking his hand. "This is your sister. It may be the last command I give, but Anna is to be afforded all the rights and powers of a princess of Avonoa. See to it the kingdom celebrates her return." He looked back and forth between the two. "Seeing the two of you together brings me more joy than I can express." He squeezed their hands with more strength than Philip had felt from him in a very long time. Then with a cough, he let them go.

"Father," Philip said, "You should rest. I'll help Anna get settled then I'm sure she'll want to return to you soon."

"Yes," Anna nodded. "I'll return quickly."

When they both stepped out of the room Philip tapped a staff-guard on the arm. "Go fetch a maidservant." Once he had gone, Philip turned back to Anna. "The King has declared that you are his daughter and I will see to it his orders are followed." He paused then tried to bore his eyes into her. "But if you ever betray this trust, I will personally see to your execution. Do you understand?"

Anna's eyes stayed locked with his for every word. "Perfectly, brother."

Philip turned to walk down the hallway. "Walk with me, sister," he said. "And tell me your story."

"It's not a long story." She stepped beside him as she spoke. "While riding in the forest my mother was thrown from her horse. The fall brought on her labor. A woman who lived in the mountains found her and helped her deliver me. As soon as she was able, my mother took on the guise of pregnancy and rode home to the castle to inform the king. She met the gray dragon along the way and was killed."

As Philip listened he strove to find holes in her story, but as it would be with simplicity, he could find none. As he had been told it, Queen Annette had been gone a few days, but that wasn't out of the ordinary. His father had gone out with a party to look for her which was out of the ordinary, but he deemed it necessary because she was so close to the time to be delivered. She had indeed been riding in the forest and when he found her she knelt in front of a dragon. The dragon breathed fire on her, killing her instantly. She had been pregnant at the time or so it had seemed. Philip hadn't spoken to his father about it much because he knew how painful it was for him. Only a year after the death of his first wife and their unborn child, Paudie had remarried Linea in order to continue the royal line.

Philip knew his father had cared deeply for his mother, but he never truly loved her as much as he loved Annette. When his second wife died after bearing a son, Paudie chose never to marry again. Unfortunately, Anna's story fit.

"Why didn't you come forward sooner?" Philip asked her. "We could've been raised together." How odd that would've been!

"When I was young," Anna answered, "Sar, the old woman, was afraid to approach our father when my mother never returned for me. Then she heard about Annette's death. She had no way to prove I was his daughter, so she decided to wait until I held some resemblance to present me to the king. As I grew older, she rationalized that she must train me as nobility before she presented me. But as I grew older still, I was frightened I might be rejected." Her voice wavered slightly. "We both put it off far too long," she finished with a whisper.

"So why did you choose now to step forward?" he asked, turning to face her.

"Our home in the mountains caught fire. Sar couldn't escape." She dropped her face as something like sorrow creased her brow. "Even my clothes burned as I barely escaped with my life. I hate to admit it, but I had nowhere else to go."

"Why didn't you step forward when our father fell ill?"

Anna snapped her head up to face Philip. "I didn't know of his illness or I would have come sooner."

"How could you not know of the king's illness?"

"We live very remote. We lived on what we could grow or hunt ourselves. We often didn't see anyone else for months at a time."

"Well," Philip said, spreading his arms wide, "you're here now." He held a hand out to the door where they'd stopped. "These will be your chambers. The inner courtyard is straight down this hall and the dining hall is to the right." As he spoke, an older woman met them in the hallway. "If you need anything, the servants will attend you. Tomorrow you will be welcomed to the kingdom as a Princess of Avonoa."

As he turned to leave, Anna called to him one last time. "Philip."

He winced. It was her right to refer to him as Philip, but very few people retained that right and even fewer used it. "Yes?" he answered her.

"Please understand," she said, "I'm your sister. We may have been raised separately, but I've always known about you and I wish to help you. I always have."

With a nod, he left her standing in her doorway. Her story was convincing and their connection undeniable, but how could he ever really trust her?

16

Ensue to Kingstor

Dak mentally beat himself with his own tail. How could he have put himself in this situation? His quarry rode right past him leaving him helpless to follow. If he bolted from the trees in daylight, the humans would hunt him down. If he waited until nightfall, his prey might escape him. How far could they possibly get in a partial day? Should he wait until dark then fly? But where? Should he go meet Tog on the mountain? He should arrive any day now. Or should he follow the human woman with Jarek?

While Dak wrestled – again – with the possibilities, the sun slid down its slope in the sky. The trees around him filled with shadow and the dark, cold air probed mercilessly. Dak had waited for night without trying. A few moments longer and the humans would go back to their homes, leaving the way clear for Dak to follow the two humans.

Suddenly the noise of wheels sounded in the distance. Dak ignored it, assuming it issued from the human village again. However, the little boy, who had earlier stepped from his little dwelling while rubbing his haunches, peered down the track of dirt past Dak. After a few more moments he yelled at the top of his lungs.

"Jarek!" he called out. "Jarek returns from Kingstor!"

Other humans sprang from their homes. The woman in the green dress heard the cries and ran out to join the others as they met horse and master. But as the box came trundling around the bend, Dak could see only one human.

The horse didn't get any further than the outer edge of the little village. Rika, Boorda, Harry, Tara, their mother and many others gathered around to hear news from Jarek. Most of them were hastily dressed or still wrapping themselves with covers. Rika approached Jarek. "What happened, Jarek?" he asked, clear and firm.

"Her name," he paused to take a deep breath, "is Princess Anna."

Dak couldn't hear anything clearly after that. All the humans began talking at once. "I knew she was nobility," one might have said. "What was she doing out there?" another whispered. "Where did she come from?" someone else asked. "I've never heard of her!" someone else sneered from the back.

Rika calmed the group and helped Jarek return to his home. "We can talk about it later," the man promised stragglers. "Let him get some rest. I'll see to your wagon, Jarek." Rika took the horse by the straps and led him around the back as Jarek and the woman in the green dress, who Dak figured must be Boorda, vanished into their home.

Dak grumbled to himself while he waited for the last few humans to get inside. But this time he couldn't wait until all the flames in the windows had died. While the humans still stirred in their homes, Dak wriggled himself free of the prickly bushes. He had to tear up one of them that clung to his back claw, but he finally stood in the same place the wagon (is that what Rika had called it?) had passed by him.

Dak heard the scuffing of feet behind him as he gazed down the track. Twisting his head around, he saw young Harry staring at him wide-eyed. Poor child, he thought to himself, I'm forced to leave you to your fate. Turning his back, he ran away from the humans.

Dak ran along the track until he came to an opening in the trees. He ripped apart the darkening sky with his black form. The human woman's scent was faint on the trail. It must be from riding in the wagon. Dak assumed they had followed this track. But to where? Kingstor? Where was that? He had no idea. But he would follow it until he had some sign of where she might be hidden.

She had to be within a half day's travel for a horse, so Dak should be able to overtake her easily. He followed the track through the mountain pass and when he emerged, he could again see the teardrop-shaped body of water in the distance.

Dak flew over small villages like the one he'd left behind. He wondered briefly if Jarek had left the woman in one of these, but then he remembered the little boy's words, "Kingstor!" 'Tor' meant 'pinnacle' in Faerie tongue, as he had learned from Betretor. Her name meant 'pinnacle of beauty'. These humble villages were no 'pinnacles of a king'.

Night spread like a veil clouding Dak's eyes. He loathed his incompetence, but he flew on. Faster and faster, he beat his wings, following the light-colored track beneath him. At times it would hide amidst snow-laden trees, but he could always find it on the other side. Once a terrified scream floated up from below, but he pressed on and the wind swept it away.

Then he saw it. The blackened backdrop of the teardrop-shaped body of water had hidden it until Dak was nearly upon it. Five tall spires rose up from a magnificent castle on the horizon to scratch at the sky. Spikes the size of a human encircled each tower making the stronghold resemble a five-legged dragon lying on its back with a spiked belly in the middle. Flags waved from one of the spikes atop each tower. In the dark he couldn't see their colors, but he could make out a shining symbol stretched across the fabric. The castle alone was nearly the size of one of its neighboring mountains. This had to be the pinnacle of a king and the only place a princess might find respite.

The wall around the castle had oversized pointed stonework atop it, matching those on a smaller wall which encircled a town directly below. Kingstor castle and the walled town sat between a rushing river and the shoreline of Teardrop Sea.

Along the track he had been following, numerous homes, animal paddocks and open fields like Jarek's followed beneath him. The larger track he had followed to Kingstor continued on from the nearest human homes on Dak's left, past the castle and walled town, alongside the river to a massive cluster of human buildings on the far side to Dak's right. There was no wall around this city and the little buildings seemed to spill out in all directions from the sea and the river. But between the two heavy human populations in front of him and directly in front of the illustrious castle, he could see the rumbling terrain of a mighty, snow-covered forest that would give him many options for cover.

Heading into this forest, Dak was relieved to find few human dwellings. Probably due to the overwhelming amount of rocks and boulders. Snow from the branches sprinkled down on him as he slipped through them to land. Here he could keep watch on the castle and its occupants. He found a place to hide surrounded by large boulders and plopped on the ground to reassess.

Flying into the castle would be ludicrous, he thought to himself. Each of those towers must have guards posted as well as the small wall surrounding the homes in front of the castle. While he might have a few hiding places, the humans would have several. He would have to be careful how he approached this fortress.

From where he sat he could see only one way the humans could access the castle. That was across the river. The track directly in front of Dak turned from the larger path to cross the river by means of a large wooden structure, ending at a massive metal and wooden barrier that, when opened, four dragons could walk through abreast. He knew there must be other ways into and out of the fortress, but he couldn't see any others from here.

Princess Anna, indeed, he snarled to himself, I'll find a way in to get her – no matter what I have to do – and wring out anything she knows.

The next day Dak awoke to a sound like a rockslide. He thought one of these wagon contraptions had been obnoxious, but numerous wheels rattling across the weather beaten bridge made his head hurt. Not just wheels and hooves crossed it either. Humans ran back and forth like they were being chased by a dragon, yelling things like, "We'll need ten more just like it!" or "Make sure William has the measurements!" or "I'm going to the square!" Even the name, "Princess Anna!" echoed among laughs. Something excited the humans around Kingstor.

Dak watched the humans all day, keeping safely to the shadows of the forest. The trees here were barely enough to hide him, but at least they wouldn't hinder him from taking flight. The boulders were his biggest asset. He could crouch behind them to hide in the snow and leap from them to gain the sky. Dak attempted to rest during the day, but always woke to more rattling of wheels or shouting from the bridge. He was easily fifteen dragon lengths away from the road, but his finely attuned hearing could pick up almost every ear-splitting sound.

There was a time around sunset when every human seemed to flock to the castle. Most of them wore blue – bright blue, the same color of the flags on the towers. As the sun cast a golden glow on the towers, a wailing issued from inside the mighty fortress. Dak squinted his sharp dragon eyes and thought he could see movement at an opening in the castle keep. Far above the ground, he might have given his wyrd he saw two humans step onto a balcony of the castle – a man and a woman, both dressed in blue. Even from this distance he could see the woman's golden hair.

He was sorely tempted to burst from his hiding place, but he knew the guards and the sheer number of humans would overwhelm him. So he sat, wedged between the boulders, to wait for the cover of darkness.

Soon enough the sun set and all the humans gathered indoors. The barrier across the river closed, but the ruckus of human voices didn't stop. It was much louder than it had been in Jarek's little village. Long into the night, humans sang and laughed and swaggered through the streets in the villages. But Dak waited patiently until even these distant sounds ceased to creep out of his hiding place.

He stretched his neck over the wide road to smell it. The passage of so many humans had covered any hint of the woman he hunted, but he knew she had to be in the castle. He had heard her name throughout the day. Some celebration of her arrival had taken place, so he assumed he would have heard if she had left as well.

A solid stone wall spanned from either side of the entrance he had been watching, along the river to the mountains on the left and the sea on the right. Dak assumed the forest contained within the wall, between the mountains and the castle, must belong to the king. Therefore, there must be more ways into the castle besides the one across the river. Dak surmised that every angle would be in the direct line of sight of at least two watch towers. But the only way he could be sure was to test his theory.

The sky was thick with clouds and the sun was long since gone. Using the darkness, Dak unfurled his wings. He heard no cries, so he took to the air. Still nothing. He lifted himself over the solid air of the river. He couldn't hover for long, so he glid over the water and the stout wall beyond.

He frightened a pasture of horses on the other side of the wall then realized unless he wanted to land among the horses, he couldn't land at all. The king's forest was thick and proud even with the bare winter branches coated in snow. The forest was almost as tall as the Black Forest, but not nearly as forbidding. Even so, he knew he would be trapped among the trees if he tried to touch down.

He flew over the forest between the castle walls and the mountains, but he briefly noticed the town within the protection of Kingstor's walls. The snow-gilded rooftops swept away from the castle with roads slanting from the direction of the forest to the front of the city. There were few breaks Dak could see in the slanted roads. He imagined if he was forced to walk through those streets unaware of the breaks, he might find himself walking all day to either the forest next to the castle or the front of the city, never reaching the castle itself. Perhaps the roads had been designed that way to keep outsiders confused.

The castle itself was the shape of an elongated pentagon, with a tower at each point. Its rooftops rose higher the further it came from the front gates. But even those were at least a dragon length higher than the rooftops of the town around it.

He continued flying, weaving from one side to the other over the treetops of the forest, always within ten dragon lengths from the mighty castle walls. Twice he saw openings in the walls around the gates, but only one opening with a gate large enough for a dragon to move through. Surrounding the high walls and towers were stretches of snow. In the summer, Dak was sure it would be covered in lush green grass. He might have been able to traverse green in the dark, but the white snow that covered it now would be in stark contrast with his black scales. So crawling in through an opening wouldn't help him.

Of course, he thought, I could always fly over the walls…Until he heard the call.

"Dragon!" a guard shouted from one of the towers. The other towers quickly echoed the call.

Dak dove below the tower watches, so when they shot their little sticks at him, they ricocheted off the unyielding scales covering his back. His wing membranes, however, were much more vulnerable. He couldn't play this risky game much longer. Luckily, the humans couldn't see any better in the dark than he could, so he flew away from the castle, back the way he had come, allowing the cries to die down behind him. This time he flew further away from the castle over the forest in front. Then, suddenly folding his wings into his sides, he dove between the branches.

He waited where he landed for most of the rest of the night, but he heard no more sounds from the humans. Near daylight, he crept back to his observation spot between the boulders.

He debated with himself again. Should he force his way into the castle grounds? Should he wait for the Anna-woman to appear on the road? Surely she could not stay in the fortress indefinitely. Except, he had heard some humans use castles for that reason occasionally. It might be moons before she'd emerge. Then he thought of Tog. Tog might already be at the attack site up the mountain, waiting for Dak to report. But to show himself around Kingstor again would most certainly put a human hunting party on his trail. No, he needed to stay where he was for now.

17

Crowning Farewell

Philip sat in a chair striving to remain regal. Anna had no such compunctions. She sat on the king's bed rumpling her gold and purple gown while stroking her father's hair. "If I had but known..." she kept repeating to herself.

The king had fallen back into unawareness of anything around him after Anna's first appearance. Philip still wondered about his father's lucidity when he had claimed Anna, but there was no way to undo his orders now.

Anna had returned to his chamber the night before after changing her clothes, and stayed with the king late into the night. She returned again first thing in the morning before breakfast. After breakfast, she met with Philip for a few minutes while he finished the preparations for their father's eventual funeral. He asked Anna if she would like to be involved in the final arrangements, but her eyes welled and she claimed she trusted Philip's decisions. She did, however, agree to sing the mourning song, traditionally sung by the women in the family who were closest to the deceased. Then she returned to her father's chamber. After the midday meal, Philip joined her to receive a report from the king's healers and majishuns.

For part of the afternoon Philip and Anna entertained visits from nobles. This time they welcomed Princess Anna bringing gifts and oaths, but Philip imagined they also hoped for invitations to the feast at the castle. Many local nobles and all the local king's guards' officers customarily attended and pledged undying fealty. Luckily for Philip, he wasn't bound to perform such ceremony, nor would he if given the choice.

Philip suspected most of the unmarried nobles wished to marry her – she was not only beautiful but her husband would be next in line for the throne. Even if he didn't like her very much, he wasn't sure if he would feed her to those wolves. Not yet, anyway. Anna received the visitors charmingly, but only stayed long enough not to be rude before she again returned to her father's chambers.

In the late afternoon Philip officiated over the short ceremonial crowning of his half-sister. Normally she would have been crowned when she was presented at the marrying age of sixteen. At that time their father would have had the honor to crown her himself. She wore the royal blue gown that only the priestess of the temple goddess Shurla was allowed to touch when she helped the royal women dress. Philip placed the crown on her head and one of the temple initiate's children gave her a ceremonial bouquet of flowers. Then Anna accompanied Philip to the balcony overlooking the inner courtyard and the square outside the castle walls to give the people of Kingstor their first look at the new princess.

That evening a grand feast was given in her honor. A young princess's presentation and crowning ceremonies were normally elaborate affairs lasting days or even weeks. Philip had heard of a princess in the Allegiant Kingdom of Avonoa who insisted her celebrations last for an entire month. Of course, the Allegiant Kingdom was actually a queendom governed by women, so Philip assumed the Heir Princess and her family desired a strong show. However, with the king so ill and Anna's appearance so sudden, Philip allowed Murthur to make all the preparations on his own.

Anna accepted everything with graceful dignity and never uttered a negative word. In fact, she commented how wonderfully prepared everything had been put together on such short notice. She handled all the ceremonies as if she had been through them all before. She sat poised. She spoke eloquently. She never batted an eyelash out of place. Philip watched for some slip, some sign of fatigue even, but grew ever disappointed by the hour. Everything went smoothly and according to custom.

The only unorthodox request was when Anna asked to leave the feasting and entertainment early so she could return to her father's side. When Philip agreed, she said a few well-composed words to the audience before she and Philip left together. Guests were allowed to stay and enjoy the entertainment while the prince and princess retired to the king's chambers.

Now, after an exhausting day, Philip wished to spend a few moments alone with his father, but Anna was always present. She spent most of her time pacing in the king's chamber, almost like a caged animal. According to the servants, she would hold the king's hand or stroke his brow for a few minutes, but more often than not she paced the length of his wall.

Anna stood from the bed. "I had hoped my return would give him strength."

"I'm sure it has," Philip assured her. "Perhaps we have yet to see the effect." This had been his own secret hope as well.

The king rolled over in his bed. Either this was very good, or very bad. The physician hurried over as Philip and Anna stood waiting. The king groaned loudly then reached his hand into the air.

Suddenly the door burst open. Philip looked up to see who intruded, but he noticed Anna kept her eyes on the king.

"Prince Philip," a captain said from the door. "I must speak to you, Sire."

Nodding to Anna's offer to stay with their father, Philip stepped into the hallway with the captain. "There had better be a dragon at the gates for this interruption."

"A black dragon, Sire," the man said. "Spotted flying over the forest by the castle wall."

Philip ground his teeth together. "Don't let word get into my father's chamber." He raced down the hallway toward the keep balcony. It would offer him a view of the sides and front of the castle. Along the way he met another captain.

"It's gone, Sire," he said. "It disappeared as quickly as it came."

"Show me where," Philip said as they walked up the stairs leading to the balcony. The first captain pushed open the door onto the veranda and all three men leaned over the rail to look.

"It appeared just over there." The first man pointed just inside the king's forest. "It flew back and forth, almost as if testing us." He pointed to one of the five towers surrounding the castle. "Tower three shot at it."

"No one saw it approach?" Philip questioned.

"No, Sire. It appeared out of nowhere."

The second captain took up the narrative. "It flew back over the wall and over the forest beyond." He pointed to the front of the castle at the forest beyond. "The guards lost sight of it over Fallon Forest."

"Did it fly away?"

"It's too dark to tell for sure, Sire, but it appeared to make haste toward the south."

"Try not to frighten anyone, but I want to know if anyone has seen any trace of a dragon in the area."

"Yes, Sire." The captains saluted then disappeared from the veranda.

After the door closed behind him, Philip stood staring into the dark night sky. "Why," he whispered to himself, "do I have the feeling the faeries have brought this evil upon us?" He gazed into the starlit sky wishing he could fly away and join Bragon in his final resting. But he knew the life of a prince and king would never be an easy one.

After bowing his head to mourn Bragon, he stood only a moment longer before the night cold forced him back indoors. When he reached the door to his father's chamber he took a deep breath before entering. The physician and Anna met him before he reached his father's bedside.

"Is everything alright?" Anna asked him.

"Yes," he lied. "All is well."

"But your father is not," the physician told him. Then he lowered his voice even more. "I'm sorry, My Liege, but I believe he only has moments left."

The old physician gathered his equipment and stepped away from the bed. Philip and Anna sat on either side of the king.

"My children," the fragile king whispered. "I'm so glad you're here." He felt on the bed for both of their hands.

"Anna," he whispered. "I want you to know..." Tears fell freely down her cheeks. "I loved your mother very much. I mourned both of you in my heart for many years. I'm so glad you've come back to us. Help your brother. He'll need you more than ever now. He'll need someone he can trust without question."

Then the old king turned to Philip. "Philip," he whispered. "You'll be a good king."

Philip couldn't trust himself to speak so he just shook his head.

"Yes," Paudie nodded. "Bragon and I have always known this. And now you'll have your sister to help you. I loved your mother too, you know. Maybe not the same way as I did Annette, but I loved her very much. And I love you, too, my son."

Philip forced a grin, but he was sure it looked more like a grimace until his father acknowledged his response. "That's better." He smiled wanly back at Philip. With a sigh, he placed both of his hands on top of his children's. Patting them repeatedly, he said, "Love will bind us." King Paudie closed his eyes, and for the first time in many months, he looked blissfully peaceful. His hands ceased. A rattle shook his chest. Then, stillness. King Paudie was dead. A heavy, mournful knell echoed in the night.

18

Honor

That day the excitement level of the humans around the castle changed. They no longer shouted or ran. Dak wondered if his appearance had subdued them this much. He watched as wagons trumbled and the humans trudged over the bridge all morning, but at midday they suddenly stopped. A strange pall fell over them when a man with a wagon stopped at the edge of the bridge and turned to gaze down the dirt path. The other humans on the bridge stopped to stare as well. A reverence hung over the humans. Dak watched in confusion at first. Then he heard wheels slowly grinding the ice and rocks lining the path.

Dak followed the human's gaze, but he couldn't see anything through the trees for a few moments.

When more wagons came into view, his brow creased in growing confusion. The humans accompanying these wagons shuffled alongside. Two women wore black veils over their faces. The men looked like the ones Dak and Tog had killed in the mountains, dressed in blue tunics with an emblem of a sword across their chests. The wagons coming up the path carried large irregularly shaped lumps on each, draped with a blue cloth diagonally emblazoned with one large sword and two smaller ones on either side. This looked like the flags that flew from the five towers. The symbol of the Noble Kingdom of the Five Swords of Avonoa.

Dak watched the man in the first wagon on the bridge remove the covering from his head as the procession passed him. Once they passed, he donned it again and went on his way.

What was that about? Dak wondered to himself.

Whatever the display had been, no one seemed alarmed about his appearance the previous night. They must have already forgotten about it, Dak assumed. Waiting here another sun cycle might cause Tog to lose his trail and thus be forced to direct the contingent elsewhere to look for Priya. Dak knew the yellow-haired human woman inside the castle knew something of Priya's whereabouts. He knew he had to find her and get the information from her, but he could hand this task over to Tog and whatever help he might bring.

I must leave tonight, he thought to himself. I'll tell Tog everything I know to aid him in the search for Priya. That should appease my wyrd to Rakgar. Dak nodded to himself satisfied he'd made the right decision, but the day dragged on.

The humans dragged on their way as well. No one spoke to each other in the streets. If they did, they didn't use more than a whisper and at this distance even Dak couldn't hear what they said. Dak finally gave up trying to learn anything else and waited for the sun to drop. Let the fresh contingent deal with it, he thought. It won't be my concern much longer.

Scratching at a small animal attempting to crawl under his scales, Dak heard a sound rarely heard. At first he assumed it was just a bee. If insects tried to get under his scales they burned to ash in an instant, so he wasn't concerned. But the sound grew louder and it was less of a buzz and more of a musical hum...Faeries.

When faeries arrived in the Rock Clouds they were welcomed as friends. They stayed in Rakgar's lair and dined privately on fresh kill. Among dragons the faeries wore only a cloak over their bodies and pliable leather skins on their feet. The sight of their translucent skin showing their flesh underneath never bothered the dragons, so the faeries kept their hoods pulled back. Now Dak could see that among humans they adhered to more modesty. Two faeries, their translucent wings thrumming the air, flew over the road and disappeared into the walled town in front of the castle. Traditional leather skins covered their feet and their dark cloaks hung down to their ankles. The cowls of their cloaks were drawn up over their heads and had a hanging positioned mid-way to cover what remained of their faces. The gloves covering their hands and arms ended out of sight under the sleeves of their cloaks.

What might this mean? Dak's mind swirled with questions. Why are the faeries here? Are the faeries helping the humans? Did they have anything to do with Priya's disappearance? Should I leave now and report this to Tog? Was Ashel's warning about the faeries right? Were the faeries untrustworthy?

Only one of the faeries carried a small bag. Dak assumed that meant their stay would be short, since humans carried loaded wagons when they traveled. After all, hadn't Jarek taken a whole wagon-load with him? And he hadn't been gone a full sun cycle.

Yes, thought Dak, these faeries must only plan to be here a short time. I can follow them when they leave. At least now he felt like he had a new course of action other than simply reporting what he knew to Tog. He could visit the faeries and try to discover their role in this disaster.

As the day wore on, Dak crept through the forest closer to the road. He didn't want to risk falling asleep and missing the faeries exit the great fortress. The trees grew thinner as he tip-taloned between them.

Soon the sparse shadows lengthened. He could rely on the darkness to blanket him once again. He could also now see the opposite side of the river. The wall around the town and the castle, taller than he could stretch his neck, protected the buildings just inside. Beyond that, the mountainous castle loomed. However, he waited well into the night and the two visiting faeries never came out of the great granite city.

19

Advocate

The impromptu funeral procession for the king's guards halted outside the gate to the inner court-yard. Philip could just make out men bringing in wagons and carts to remove bodies (or perhaps just parts) from the piles on the wagons. Women and children were kept well away from the gruesome sight. The thirty men he had sent into the mountains had been slaughtered and it was entirely his fault.

Philip ground his teeth together and wrenched himself away from the window. "You there," he pointed to a guard standing in the hall. "Find the faeries Kradik and Ortym in the village outside Kingstor. Bring them here immediately."

The guard saluted with a fist on his chest then swept down the hall. Philip made his way to the audience chamber with Murthur following close behind. Upon entering the room he noticed the thick black cloth stretched diagonally over his father's portrait. He could just see his father's eyes staring over the ebony bow.

Philip forced his eyes away. He stepped lightly to his throne on the right of his father's, but before he took his seat, Murthur spoke.

"Sire," he whispered, "that is no longer your place."

Philip paused, leaning with his hand on the arm of the throne. Luckily, there was no scheduled court audience. Courtiers weren't watching his every move, waiting for a sign of weakness like wolves outside a rabbit hole. Every move he'd taken today had been a struggle. But he forced himself on. "You're right, of course." He pulled his hand away and turned to the more ornate throne. Taking this one last step up was the most difficult he'd taken in his life.

When he'd finally seated himself on the king's throne for the first time, he tilted his head in Murthur's direction. "Thank you," the new king told his servant. "Thank you for your loyalty." Murthur nodded, then took his place behind the king's throne before the doors to the audience chamber opened.

Philip's head hung. Must I attend to business now? he lamented to himself. Won't these pestering nobles ever leave me be?

But when he lifted his head, a more welcome sight met his eyes than ever before. "Torgon?" Philip asked in surprise. "What are you doing here so soon? You should be with your family."

Torgon knelt in front of the king with his fist to his chest. "My mother has my two younger siblings to comfort her. She felt, as I do, that it is my duty as your friend to sustain you in your own grief."

Philip could hold back no longer. His eyes welled and his heart seemed to seize. He made no motion, but his ever faithful servant immediately cleared the room of the guards and followed them out. After a moment, Philip stepped down from the dais toward Torgon. "You're my friend?" he asked.

Torgon stood and looked him in the eye. "I don't know if you remember the few times we hunted together when we were younger. We were just shadows of our father's friendship, but I cherish those memories."

"I do remember," Philip answered.

"I will always be your friend."

Philip finally allowed drops to spill from his eyes. This morning he felt so alone and vulnerable. He couldn't imagine filling the role his father had done for so many years. But now, with the support of just one friend alongside him, he felt the weight of the king-dom lift slightly from his shoulders. He collapsed on the steps leading up to his throne and allowed himself to grieve.

"Sire," Torgon sat next to him on the floor, "you can't hold a kingdom together while you fall to pieces."

"He was..." Philip said while attempting to stem the flow of tears, "...he was the only family I've ever known."

Torgon gestured toward the door. "At least you have more family now."

Philip gave an extremely un-royal snort. "Her? She's not family...she's..." His voice trailed off.

"An imposter?"

"No." Philip shook his head. "But a liar to be sure." He wiped his nose on a handkerchief from his pocket, something Murthur would never have allowed him to do in front of others. "How can I ever trust her when the only thing I feel every time I look at her is that she's keeping something from me?"

"Then," Torgon threw his arms wide, "you're stuck with me."

Philip grinned genuinely for the first time in a long time. "Really? Will you take over the kingdom for me, then?"

"Well," Torgon hemmed as his face and arms dropped, "think of me more as the older brother who never takes responsibility, but takes orders very well." The two young men sat in silence for a few moments at the foot of the thrones. Then Torgon lifted his head. "I heard you demoted Murzod after I left." Philip could hear the grin in his voice without looking at him.

"The man is an arrogant fool." Philip stuffed the handkerchief back into his pocket. "But I think I allowed my frustration of the moment to run away with me."

"Or perhaps you should listen to your instincts more often."

Philip looked up again. He wasn't sure if he'd said it in jest, but it felt good to hear nonetheless. "Perhaps," he echoed.

"You're a strong man and you'll be a strong king." Torgon reached a hand out to Philip, who gratefully accepted it. He easily hoisted Philip from his seat on the steps.

"Sire?" a timid voice came from the great double doors. Murthur peeked his head through.

"It's alright, Murthur." Philip waved him in. "On to business."

Murthur nodded and opened the doors. He came to stand behind the king. Two guards took their posts on either side of the throne dais. A few nobles – the hawks that always seemed to know when something noteworthy is happening – tiptoed in to watch proceedings. Torgon took his place standing at the right arm of the king and two more guards took their positions next to the doors.

Philip took notice of this moment. Although he wasn't wearing a crown (he wasn't in the habit of it) and Torgon still wore the tunic with two swords on it, which symbolized a lieutenant's rank, these were the positions they would fill for the rest of their lives.

He was just wondering if he should tell the guards to remove his old throne when the faeries walked in the doors.

"Your Majesty wished to see us?" Kradik said bowing slightly at the waist.

"Yes," Philip's memory served to renew the anger he felt about the slaughtered men. "A dragon flew around the castle last night. Did you know of it?"

"Yes, Sire."

Philip struggled to keep his temper in check with these beings around. "You claimed to be the experts on dragons. Is it normal for them to test the limits of their enemies?"

The faeries looked at each other then turned back to the king. "At times, Sire," Kradik answered. "Many species have a habit of methodically testing boundaries."

"Do you, in your expert opinions, think we should expect an attack from this black dragon?" he asked.

"It's possible, Sire," Ortym answered.

"Possible?" Philip's voice rose. "Aren't you supposed to know the future?"

Kradik's cowl lowered slightly at the insinuated insult. "The future is a complex web to untangle, Sire," he said. "It is by no means easy nor thorough."

"Then what can you tell me?" Philip asked again.

"The dragon might be territorial after the first attack," Ortym answered.

Through thinned lips, Philip asked, "Did you know this would happen?"

"No, Sire," Kradik said.

"But we have a way to prevent any attack," Ortym offered.

Philip sat up straighter in his chair. "And how is this?"

Kradik held out a hand. In it sat a small yellow bird with brown spots, no bigger than a hummingbird, and a small phial with a white powdery substance in it. The bird made no attempt to escape, but sat in the faerie's palm looking boldly at the king. "We know how to locate him and we have the means to capture him."

20

Questioning

Even if the temperature hadn't dropped dangerously low in the night, Dak still wouldn't have rested well. He stirred all night, waking at the slightest sounds around him. With his sensitive ears he heard night animals prowling, but when they felt the dragon's heat, they withdrew. Being on edge all night made Dak sure he would have heard the faeries if they had come or gone, but they remained behind the walls all night.

The silence was maddening. Finally, Dak couldn't resist the urge to search the area. He knew the tower guards would see him if he wandered too close to the castle or the grounds around it, so instead he backtracked through the forest before he took to the sky.

From what he could see in the night sky, there were a cluster of human dwellings nearby and cleared fields like Jarek's dotting the countryside. The path the humans used wound its way further on between the mountains to Jarek's village.

Dak figured he could learn nothing of Rakgar's daughter by surveying these puny human dwellings. He knew the magnificent fortress shielded the secrets he sought. Thus he decided to cross the threshold of the castle's walls nearest the mountains furthest from the towers.

Dak fought against the wind as he stayed as close as possible to the mountains. He saw no signs of humans this far from their path. Dak scanned the mountainsides next to him, but saw nothing in the darkness. The only problem with using the darkness to cover him was that it could also cover a foe.

He slipped over the wall where it met the mountain next to what must have been a mighty waterfall in the summer. Once he was over the wall, he dove down into the trees. Silently he watched and waited. The only sound he heard was the wind whistling through the desolate boughs.

Looking at the landscape, he could see why a human monarch might use this area if he were bound to the dirt. Any approaching enemy would lose men trying to cross the mountain cliffs here. The fathomless river and Teardrop Sea enclosed from the other sides, making it nigh on impossible to approach the castle without bridge or boat. Even the mountain range beyond the forest seemed impassable without wings.

Dak crept through the trees away from the deserted falls. This forest was like all the others he had seen so far. He was sure it would be abundant with life and creatures of all kinds in summer. He couldn't imagine why it was contained within the wall protecting the city and its castle, but, again, there was no information about Priya to be gained here.

With a low growl and a gnashing of teeth, Dak took to the air again. He didn't fly so close to the castle walls as to alert the guard again, but he didn't skirt the wall and city as carefully as when he had come.

Let them find me, he grumbled to himself. Perhaps tomorrow I'll fly straight into the city and thrash their king until I get information.

The ground shook slightly as he slammed four claws into the soil beneath the trees on his return to his watch post. The night wore on, but Dak didn't notice. Instead, he attempted to unravel the web of what he knew. Priya was gone, by majikal means to be sure. There was no other way she would have disappeared so completely. Tog hadn't shown up yet, but it was just a matter of time.

Do I wait and watch longer, thought Dak, or do I attack the humans and ask questions of any momentary survivors? What would my father do? What would Tog or Priya expect me to do? What would Rakgar have me do?

21

Relations

Delicate golden forks with intricate patterns sculpted along the handles gently clinked on porcelain plates. Succulent meats and fruits adorned the table alongside fluffy golden breads and steaming soups and sauces. But even with three crystal goblets, whose contents had already been filled at least twice, the conversation ran dry. Until four days ago the occupants of this royal dining table had been lifelong friends. Now the relationships gathered were as new and fragile as the laced candy around the pudding.

The day had been the busiest Philip had ever known. He insisted the faeries stay in the castle to plan the dragon capture with him. He had sat with them for hours to ensure he could anticipate anything that might happen, but he still felt as if they were keeping something from him. They refused to dine with him, saying they had much to prepare, but Philip felt as if they had no desire.

Also this day he made final preparations for his official coronation, which wouldn't take place for more than a month. By that time all the nobles could gather to witness and the four other kings and queens of the Five Swords of Avonoa could either send representatives to renew their alliance or join him themselves.

Finally, they had laid his father to rest after a beautiful ceremony followed by a slow march under the castle church to the catacombs. Anna had wept appropriately, but never stumbled once on the death march. Her eyes seeped at all the right moments during her mourning song, but she performed it majestically. Philip had been forced to admire her sturdy constitution. If her tale was true, then she had watched the woman who raised her die in a fire only to meet and lose her own long lost father within a few days. Philip's heart softened slightly – despite his misgivings – at the thought of her poignant story.

During the ceremony, Philip had also come to accept the loss of his father. He would miss him terribly, but at least he had a close friend in Torgon to advise him now. His father had fought his illness for so long; Philip couldn't be sad thinking the pain had finally ended.

Now Philip sat at the head of the royal dining table, wearing a traditional black mourning sash across his chest. Anna sat at Philip's right, her rightful place as princess. She wore a black mourning gown with an extra thick trim of black lace around the bottom hem and wrists. Most of the royal gowns in the castle had to be altered in such a manner to fit her tall stature. Her long yellow locks curled up tightly against her head and the black veil she wore over her face all day was thrown back to allow her to eat and drink. It was traditional for all in mourning to wear black, but women were also required to cover their faces and hair when someone they loved died. Philip wondered briefly when he first saw her this morning whether her maid had informed her of the funeral traditions upheld by royals, or if Anna had already known.

Torgon sat across from Anna on Philip's left with the same black mourning sash. If only Anna weren't here, Philip mused for a moment. He had much more in common with Torgon. They could discuss growing up in the shadow of great men with Bragon's guidance. Torgon was close to Philip's age as well and he felt this could only bond them further. But things were very different from what they might have been when he had been just a prince.

"Philip," Anna said, interrupting his introspection. He couldn't help wincing when she said it. "I'm sorry," she paused. "Would you prefer I not call you 'Philip'?"

Torgon almost buried his nose in his potatoes.

"You're well within your rights to call me what you please," Philip answered without looking at her.

"I can tell it makes you uncomfortable. I'll address you however you desire."

Philip took a breath. "You may call me 'Philip', Anna." He took a sip of his wine. "As well as yourself, Torgon."

Torgon's mouth was full of potato so he simply nodded and raised his glass.

Anna continued her address. "Very well, Philip, as I started to say, my maid has gone missing," she said.

Philip glanced at the skirt hovering behind her. "Then who is that?"

Anna grinned good-naturedly. "Her replacement. My maid and I went out to the forest yesterday. She claimed the need to return to the castle for thicker clothing, but never returned."

"Did you ask the guards if they'd seen her?"

"Yes," she said. "They said she never returned to the castle. She's well on in years, Philip. I fear for her."

"I'll have the guards search for her," he said. "Will that put your mind at ease?"

"Yes," she answered with a smile. "Thank you."

"Speaking of 'years', Torgon, I meant to ask your age," Philip said. "Murzod complained of one 'so young' to receive such an appointment, so it made me curious. You don't seem much older than myself."

Torgon swallowed. "I'm nineteen, Si... – er, Philip."

"Very young for a lieutenant," Anna said, "let alone a royal general."

Philip grinned, but Torgon answered. "When I was a staff-guard, I saved a captain's life while hunting. He insisted I be promoted to lieutenant." He shifted his eyes to Philip. "My father didn't know about my promotion until after it happened."

"I remember him mentioning it," Philip nodded.

"You must be a very accomplished swordsman," Anna said.

Torgon shifted a shoulder. "I'd like to think so."

"But one can't be promoted unless they pass a test of skill, isn't that true?" she asked them. "Unless by the king, of course."

"Yes," Torgon answered. "I had passed it long before. When the captain heard, he joined with another captain to promote me on the spot."

Philip stared at Anna through narrowed eyes. As they spoke, she picked up exactly the right utensil from among the array before her on the table. She held it the right way. She sat the right way. She spoke the right way. "I don't understand," he finally said to her. "How do you know these things?"

"What things?" she asked.

"How the royal chain of command works? How the ladder of promotion works? How royalty should conduct themselves?"

"I told you," she said. "I was trained as a noble."

"But how?" Philip leaned forward in his high-backed chair. "How is it an old woman living in the mountains with little to no contact to the outside world knew how to train you in the ways of nobility?"

Anna shook her head. "She didn't train me."

"Then who?" Philip asked. "You can't tell me a noblewoman trained you." He looked to Torgon for help in explaining. "No lord or lady would train an unknown – a commoner – in nobility. They would rather die than degrade themselves in such a manner."

"Forgive me, Philip," Anna said, "but you fail to acknowledge the capabilities of an entire class of your kingdom."

The confusion on Torgon's face proved to Philip he wasn't the only one who didn't understand. He put his fork down with a little more force than he intended. "Who trained you?"

"Who trained you to be royalty?" she asked, without lifting her eyes from her plate.

"My – our father, of course."

Anna lifted her eyes to his. "No, he didn't."

"Of course he did."

"No," she shook her head. "He was ever present, and probably encouraging and supportive, but he wasn't the one person to train you."

"He…" Philip's response hung in his mouth. She was right. "No," he leaned back in his chair, "now that you mention it…" Torgon's eyes bounced between the two royals. "Murthur," Philip finally said quietly.

"Yes, My Lord," his servant said, stepping forward.

"No, no, no." Philip waved him off without looking at him. "The answer to her riddle." He grinned at Anna. "A servant trained you."

"Yes," she smiled back. "Servants and commoners are more capable than you might be aware."

Torgon glanced sideways at the guards standing by the door to the dining hall. "But what do you suggest they're capable of doing?"

"As much as you or I," Anna answered as she picked up her goblet. But the raised eyebrows of the two men were enough to show their doubt. "It's true," she insisted. "For instance, Philip, if you were to divulge to Torgon and me some fantastic secret of the kingdom at this moment, who would hear it?"

"Yourself and Torgon, of course."

"But you forget, your servant stands behind you, my servant stands behind me and two guards stand at the door." She held up four fingers. "You don't even notice their presence, but they would take your secret to the next world, if necessary. Yet, if they overhear something that might not require secrecy – and they know the difference – the whole kingdom knows it in almost the next instant."

"Being a dreadful gossip is hardly what I would consider capable," Torgon chortled.

"Perhaps," Philip agreed. "But a marvelous communication system, no doubt."

"Fine," Anna said, turning back to her food, "but Philip, I wonder if you're even aware that Murthur is not in the room at this moment."

Philip shifted his head only slightly to see his servant's legs standing still behind him. "Noble effort, Anna."

But Anna grinned wider. "Sir," she addressed the man behind Philip, "what is your name?"

Silence.

"Have no fear," Philip said over his shoulder while keeping his eyes on her, "answer the princess."

Another moment passed before the servant responded, "My name is Ruthur, Your Highness."

Philip vaulted from his chair, almost knocking it over in the process. He tried to look the man in the face, but the servant dropped his eyes at the gesture. "Look at me," Philip said sternly.

"Nay, Sire, I shan't." The servant continued to avoid the king's gaze. It only frustrated Philip more to see that his hair and the traditional tilted headpiece made him look exactly like Murthur.

"Look at me, I say!" Philip demanded.

The servant finally acquiesced, but only for a moment. Philip narrowed his eyes at the man. He was clean-shaven with a long, straight nose and pointed chin. He found nothing remarkable about the man. Finally, he turned away from him and regained his seat.

"I'm sorry, Your Majesty," Ruthur mumbled. "I didn't mean to upset you."

"You didn't upset him," Anna said. Her grin hadn't moved. "It bothers him that he doesn't even know what Murthur looks like."

Philip put both hands flat on the table to steady himself. "Where is Murthur?"

"He fell ill this morning, My Lord," Ruthur offered. "I'm his younger brother. It's my place to serve you in his stead. I'm sure he'll be back in the morning."

"Have you stood in for him before?" Philip asked the table.

"Yes, Sire," Ruthur answered. "Why, I served you in Murthur's name just the day before the faeries arrived in the kingdom, and many other occasions as well."

"You..." Philip hesitated. "You also trained me as a royal, then?"

"Yes, Sire," Ruthur said tenderly. "'Twas I who encouraged you to pursue your practice with the bow, Sire."

Philip turned again to look at the man as if he'd never seen him before, which he hadn't. He searched out the man's eyes, but only held them for a brief moment.

"The bow, Philip?" Anna asked.

"My weapon of choice," he explained, without looking away from the man.

"I've heard of your incredible expertise with a bow as well," Torgon put in. "You can out-shoot any man in the five kingdoms."

"I noticed your proficiency as well as your enjoyment when you used it, and I encouraged you one day to find more time to practice," Ruthur said. "I'm sorry if I've caused you any ill feelings, Sire."

"No, Ruthur," Philip said, "don't be sorry. I'll never forget the advice. Nor regret following it."

"Thank you, Sire," Ruthur whispered to the floor.

"Rather capable, wouldn't you say?" Anna sipped her wine.

"Yes," Philip sat up straighter. "Very capable. Ruthur, you're to announce yourself when standing in for Murthur from now on. Is that clear?"

"Yes, Sire."

"And yet you will not deign to look in their eyes," Anna said, shaking her head.

"That's how it has always been done," Philip answered, picking up his fork again.

"Just because something has always been done the same way doesn't mean it couldn't stand improvement," Anna said. Philip and Torgon both stopped moving to stare up at her. "What did I say?" she questioned them.

"My father," Torgon said, "used to say something very similar. He said, 'The title "tradition"....'"

"'...doesn't make it law,'" Philip finished the saying.

"A wise man." Lifting her goblet, she said, "To General Bragon. May his wisdom live forever in those who practice it."

22

Beguiled

As a new sun cycle dawned, Dak wrestled silently with his many questions. The slow trickle of humans began again on the bridge in front of him. At first he ignored the puny beings and their frail plights. But before the heat of the distant sun could bring him any comfort for the day, he heard a rhythmic tromping start from behind the city wall in the distance.

The mighty gates of Kingstor city opened to issue forth two human men on horseback. Their beasts' hooves cantered in time as their riders shouted to clear the way in front of them.

Behind them followed four columns of men marching in step. Their tunics all bore the blue crest of Avonoa and swords hung at their sides. Humans, beasts and wagons scurried out of their way as they crossed the bridge over the river. The columns of men ran ten rows deep before two more men on horseback ended the procession.

At the head of the bridge where it intersected the larger road, one horse and rider turned to Dak's left, toward the forest and villages; the other horse and rider turned the other direction and followed the path around the far side of the forest toward the sprawling city by the sea. Two columns of soldiers followed the first horseman and the other two columns followed the other. Dak realized with growing concern that soon forty-four human guards would be on either side of him.

He closed his eyes to listen carefully as the sound of marching boots continued on the beaten paths. A bird chirruped in a nearby tree, making the sound difficult to hear, but Dak strained his senses to follow the boots.

Then the humming of faerie wings started again.

Of course, thought Dak, they would come out while the sun is in the sky, when I can't follow them nor even approach them for help.

Dak relaxed his coiling haunches and growled in frustration.

The bird in the tree chirruped louder as the faeries did something Dak hadn't expected. Without a word to each other they, too, separated at the head of the bridge and followed the path in two different directions around the forest.

They must be following the men, Dak assumed. But why?

The bird's noise reached a pitch so shrill it pierced Dak's ears like daggers. He couldn't hear the humming or marching with the racket, so he lifted his upper body, gradually settling on his back legs behind the speckled yellow creature. The trees didn't offer much darkness to cover him, but the men and the faeries were nowhere in sight and the docile little bird didn't seem to notice his measured movements.

His claws clamped around it so quickly the bird didn't have time to turn. Dak tossed the tiny morsel into his mouth and swallowed it whole. Then, sliding back to the ground, he listened for movement.

Both the humming and the tromping had ceased, but Dak couldn't be sure if the men had stopped suddenly or if they had marched too far away for him to hear. Dak raised his head slightly, then turned his head to the right. With his eyes closed he begged his ears to find something to hear. He twisted his head to the left then tilted it down. The only sound he heard was the gentle winter wind freezing the snow on the branches overhead.

Dak sighed. The humans must have moved on and taken his chance to follow the faeries with them. Before opening his eyes again, Dak inhaled deeply through his nostrils.

The wind carried a moist, salty odor with it. Dak hadn't missed this stench while he had been hiding in the woods, but he recognized it instantly. Human men.

Then came the unmistakable sound of human boots crunching over the thin coating of snow on the forest floor. Dak's eyes snapped open. Looking to his left he saw in the distance a boot sticking out from a bush, a sword tip hovering over a rock and a human hand on the side of a tree trunk. Hiding throughout the forest a row of twenty-two men stretched along his left side and conceivably behind him as well.

He knew where the other men were, but he had to look anyway. Slowly turning to his right, he saw distinct proof that he was surrounded by more than forty men. This had to be the faeries' doing. How else would these brainless bipeds know where to find him?

Even the ice seemed to stop and stare. Dak's belly burned with anger. He could possibly run toward the castle, but he must assume there were more guards stationed behind the wall for the same purpose, or even hidden by the river or bridge. He couldn't take to the air without his wings immediately being shot through. He could fight his way out, but then he would never get any answers.

He raised his top lip and growled into the forest, not bothering to mask the sound this time. A movement to his left caught his eye and he heard a whisper, "Allow me to go first."

A moment later one of the faeries stood from behind the shrubbery. The cowl of his cloak covered his face. As he lifted his wings to set them humming, Dak heard more humming echo from the other side of the ranks of men.

Dak watched as they drew near. Looking back and forth between the two faeries, the words of Ashel came back to him. "Dak," she had said, " – the faeries are not to be trusted."

The two faeries hovered in front of him, close enough for the humans' useless ears not to hear their words.

"My friend," the faerie on the left whispered, "let us help you."

His words sounded hollow. Emotionless. They kept their hands in their side pockets so all he could see other than their cloaks was their feet dangling in the air.

"Unless we stop them … together … " the other faerie whispered.

"…these men will kill you."

"You need only ask our help," the faerie goaded him.

Dak knew that the faeries knew the dragon laws as well as he did. If the humans heard him speak a single word to the faeries, the spells that bound them and held the whole of Avonoa in balance would be broken. Or such was the belief. Dak would be forced to kill the faeries and all the humans, but only if he could. Ashel had been right. At least these two faeries could not be trusted.

Baring his teeth, he growled again. Louder this time.

The two faeries flew backward slightly at the threat, but came back again. Turning to each other, one said, "Let it be as it must," then he nodded.

The other faerie turned to face the mighty black dragon and produced a gloved hand from inside his cloak. Dak only had time to open his mouth before the enemy blew a fistful of dust into his face. He tried to lift his claw, but it felt as if the weight of a boulder held it down. The trees and snow blended together in a mass of gray and white before Dak fell unconscious upon it.

⁓

The sound of heavy boots strode briskly down the hall. The eager boy had presented himself in the king's audience hall only moments ago, but Philip couldn't contain his excitement. When he'd sent the men out with the faeries to ensnare the dragon, he dared not hope they would succeed so quickly. Perhaps his suspicion of the faeries had been premature and they would indeed serve as useful allies against the dragons.

Philip brushed past the guards trying to warn him that the castle balcony had not been secured. He couldn't wait. He fumbled with the latch. He'd never opened it for himself before, but he couldn't wait for someone to do it. Most of the servants already hung out of adjacent windows. This one was reserved for royalty. Finally, the handle sprung open and the iron-clad floor-to-ceiling windows that served as the balcony doors swung silently open on their well-oiled hinges.

The young king rushed to the edge of the balcony. The overlook was usually used for royal announcements or proclamations, but now it would be used for royal craning.

Below the ornate balcony lay the keep courtyard encircled by the keep walls. Outside spread the city within the great walls. The city streets crowded with people surrounding an undulating mass being carried through the streets. Two carts held together by majik from the faeries held the massive black creature being drawn through the courtyard's arched gateway.

A black dragon, as dark as a moonless night, was wrapped in thick, majikally reinforced chains. Philip watched in awe as twenty men shoved the enormous lump from the two carts, dumping it unceremoniously onto the snow-covered lawn in the courtyard.

He stared, elated, as Torgon saluted and the men bowed to him. He had secretly worried he would never be able to recover from the failed attack on the dragons. He worried the dragons his men had killed would come back from the World of Souls to haunt his kingdom. But this was no spirit. This creature was flesh and blood. He could therefore use it as a symbol for his reign.

23

Temptation

Whenever Dak awoke, like many dragons he had the habit of keeping his eyes closed in order to take in the sounds and smells around him first. Occasionally he woke in the middle of the night forcing his other senses to work harder than his eyes so the habit had been reinforced over time. This time was no different.

This time Dak's nostrils flared at the smell of humans. Disgusting. But there was also the strong mineral scent of stone, lots of stone. The last thing he could remember, he had been in the forest. There had been a few boulders around him, but not this much. Now, he could catch the slight smell of hibernating plants and a little more dirt, cloth, like the faeries or humans wear, but the scent of unyielding rock overpowered them by far.

He also heard the murmur of human voices. In the forest, he had been far enough from the humans not to hear their mutterings, but now they were – then he remembered – surrounding him!

Terror built in his belly, boiling into his throat, threatening to choke him. Now he remembered – The humans. Forty-four of them. The faeries. Untrustworthy. Only two. But two was enough. It only took one fistful. Vile faeries!

Dak's eyes snapped open. Pointed merlons hovered over his head on the three sides he could see, making him feel like he sat on the tongue in the gaping jaws of a monstrous dragon. The smooth angles of the curved stone were obviously designed to discourage large, clawed, winged animals from landing on them. Columns as thick as a man ran around the entire perimeter covering a tunnel-like structure. A man might be able to walk atop it, but only the most desperate of dragons (or the smallest) might manage it.

In one direction Dak could see through the columns on both sides of the covered walkway to the white treetops of the forest. In the opposite direction, on the other side of the courtyard, he could see through the columns to Teardrop Sea. Above him he could barely make out a balcony jutting out over his head and supported by stone walls embossed with intricate patterns of the sun and moon wrapped with ivy and swords. He lay in a courtyard of the castle keep, on a swath of brown grass. The warmth from his body had melted the snow around him. The dirt and grass under him had begun to soften and felt like the fatty tissues from a fresh kill. But majikal chains encircled his body and snout. The chains wrapped around his four legs as well, binding him much the same way Tog had been bound on the mountain.

Tog. By the One! Dak thought, where is Tog? Perhaps he'll steal into the keep in the middle of the night. In the same thought he realized, No, simple animals don't rescue each other, do they? That's why we were forced to kill all the men who captured Tog. We can't kill everyone in this castle. I'm on my own.

With that thought he shook at the shackles around his feet. Not only did they hold fast, but they didn't allow for anything but the smallest of movements. He could feel the chains against his back cutting into his wings. Even his tail was bent sharply back against his body and restrained. His head was chained on both sides to stakes in the ground. To escape, at least one of the chains holding him would have to be broken.

As he tested the restraints, he heard the drumming of feet about the columns surrounding the courtyard. "It's awake! It's awake!" he heard men yelling. "To your posts! Don't get too close!" someone else shouted.

Guards posted themselves next to the columns on the edge of the courtyard more than a dragon's length away from Dak on all sides. He could only assume there were more men posted behind him. Each man held a long stick of wood with three sharp points angled on the top of it. A pike, Dak thought he had heard the human weapon called.

Straining against them told Dak his bonds would not break. He even tried to twist his head around to burn the chains with his fire, but he couldn't turn in any direction.

How did I get myself into this? He mourned to himself. I never should've left the Rock Clouds. Evil Faeries!

With the men at their posts more footsteps sounded behind them, along with the humming Dak recognized. The faeries entered the courtyard beside a tall young man. This day, his dark brown hair was encompassed with a circlet of silver. The circlet itself was adorned with miniscule crossed swords and a bright blue gem situated on his forehead. His harsh jawline had no trace of the fur Dak had seen on other men. Despite his youthful appearance, the young man carried himself regally, with a straight back and squared shoulders. His penetrating blue eyes under heavy overhanging eyebrows seemed to reach into your soul and pull out every secret. Even without the silver crown, Dak could tell this young man was royalty. He swept a heavy fur cloak around his shoulders as he marched into the courtyard.

The faeries' hoods were drawn up and gloves covered their hands, the way they appeared among humans. But Dak could feel their eyes on him as they stilled their wings to steal into the courtyard.

Treacherous faeries! Dak growled to himself. This must be how they captured Priya! But where is she?

"My coronation approaches," the regal young man said as he stared at the mighty black beast in front of him. "Can we do it then?"

"Possibly, King Philip," One of the faeries spoke, but it was hard to tell which.

"There is a simple way to guess the timing." The other faerie spoke and Dak was almost certain it was the one on the left.

King Philip looked at the two then nodded. "Of course," he said knowingly. He turned to one of the guards in the courtyard who didn't have a pike, only a sword. "Captain, bring in the goat."

A goat? Dak thought. These humans really are mad!

The captain disappeared for only a few moments before he returned with a small brown goat. He led the animal by a rope into the courtyard. Warily, he shoved the goat in front of Dak's nose with his foot. It smelled good, but Dak kept wondering about the point of this exercise. Were they trying to feed him? Did they want to keep him as a pet?

The goat stood bleating once in a while, looking from man to man to beast. Dak looked at them, too. The men watched. The faeries watched.

I thought humans were at least smarter than this, Dak wondered. Or at least the faeries.

The goat bleated again. No longer fearing Dak it reached over to smell him. Dak twitched his own nose. As mouthwatering as the goat smelled, he was more frustrated by its presence than hungry. He wished he could figure out what these men expected him to do.

The goat eventually nodded its head to playfully butt against Dak's nostril. This was going too far. He tried to pull away from the creature, but the chains held him fast. The ridiculous animal butted him again. This time Dak could take no more. He didn't do much. He simply exhaled scalding hot air to scare the pest away.

It worked, but only momentarily. The goat jumped backward, as most animals do from a dragon's breath, but otherwise didn't run. The men around him, however, had a strange reaction.

"There! You see!" the young king said triumphantly, gesturing to Dak for the faeries' benefit.

"Perhaps," said the first faerie.

The king shook his head and waved to the goat. "Remove it."

But this was the chance Dak had truly been waiting for. As the captain stepped forward to take the goat's leash his leg crossed in front of Dak's nostril. A momentary roar of flame leapt from his nose, engulfing the goat and half of the human.

With a howl of pain the man stumbled to Dak's side, away from his snout. Two other men ran to his aid, slapping him with their coats to put out the fire. The fledgling king's brow creased with anger.

"Now you see, My Lord," the second faerie said, "They are....more....clever....than you might think." The spell binding the faeries' tongues from revealing the dragons' intelligence asserted itself over his words.

He struggled against the force of the spell punctuating his speech. This reminded Dak that no matter what they said, human or faerie alike, he must not respond.

King Philip clenched his fist next to his leg as he watched the injured man carried away. "How long must we wait?"

"It's difficult to say, Your Highness," one faerie said. "Judging by this," he nodded in the direction of the scorch marks and the charred goat remains, "this dragon must have recently eaten. It will take at least a few weeks for his fire to die down. Another two after that and his fire will begin to consume him. You won't be able to kill him until then. But it might be sooner for the winter."

King Philip nodded. "Are you sure you can keep his body from turning to ash?"

No! Dak's heart constricted. They can't be that cruel! The faeries know a dragon's soul can never return to the World of Souls unless its body turns to embers!

"Yes, Your Majesty," the second faerie said. "We are the best shaman for the spell."

"How can you be sure his fire won't consume him before we kill him?" the king asked.

"We can perform other tests at the appropriate time to ensure it," the first faerie said. "We'll begin those in three weeks' time."

The king nodded. "How soon will you harvest from him?"

Harvest?! Dak's eyes almost popped open at the word, but he managed to pass it off as a blink. Dragons are the most highly majikal creatures in the world. He knew majishuns and shamans bartered for dragon parts and pieces. Their scales, tears, bones, even blood and ashes were used to work powerful majik. But some of these, particularly parts of the body, turned to ash once severed so they were rare ingredients to gather.

"We won't take anything until moments before we actually kill him," the first faerie said.

"Of course," the second faerie took a step forward, "If we kill him the right way, we'll get more from the process."

"No," the regal boy stared fearlessly into the dark folds of the faeries' cowls before him. Without hesitation, he continued. "This will be the defining moment of my kingship." He turned to glare at the black dragon. "I will kill him myself," he said, before turning back to the faeries. "My way."

—

After hearing these plans Dak didn't get much rest. The king must have given everyone in his kingdom leave to torment him because they came in droves. Small ones, large ones, round ones, thin ones. Men, women, youth and children. Some would bring animals, most brought large sticks or rocks. They marched by him in lines and took turns poking, prodding, pushing, hitting, throwing, kicking, scratching or anything else they could think of. All the while the guards stood with their pikes off to the side, laughing.

In the evenings the guards made a sick game out of who could run up, kick him in the snout then get away without getting burned. Dak singed a few of them, but they came at him from the side where he couldn't see and they always did it as he drifted off to sleep. He knew they were trying to get him to use up his fire faster, but he couldn't react naturally to their provocation without them knowing he understood their strategy.

One night, after a particularly brutal day, one of the faeries crept into the courtyard. Before he stepped onto the brown grass he stood on the fringes muttering silky words into the air. Then he slowly approached.

"Don't be alarmed, dragon," he whispered. "I've come to talk." Dak didn't bother looking at him. He wanted to ask what they had done with Priya – he wanted to force answers from them, but he knew he couldn't react in the slightest.

As if reading his mind, the faerie said, "Don't worry. You're free to speak. I've cast a spell around us so we won't be heard." Dak's eyes turned to him for a moment, but quickly shifted back to the ground. Ashel's warning echoed loudly in his ears.

"My name is Kradik," he said. "I'm a faerie shaman. I have the power to save you if you'll only trust me."

Dak sighed and closed his eyes.

"Do you know the story of the faerie curse, dragon?" Kradik asked.

Dak held still. He didn't know the whole story, but he had a feeling he was going to hear it.

"You probably know that a faerie gave the first dragon the gift of speech. But as this wondrous gift spread among the dragons, they begged the faeries never to tell the humans about their intelligence."

That wasn't the way Dak had heard the story told. He'd been taught that the faeries felt guilty for changing the course of a species and didn't want to tell anyone else.

"The faeries swore on their lives never to tell a soul." Kradik paused. "But it wasn't sufficient for the self-righteous dragons."

Dak wondered if Kradik knew that dragons pass memories between themselves and their children. The memory of the faerie council issuing a decree to bind all the faeries' tongues hardly sounded to Dak like they were forced.

"A faerie council member was obliged to work a spell to bind the tongues of all faeries for all time, until the time the dragons chose to end the spell."

Dak didn't know the specifics of the spell.

"If I walked over to the guard and told him of your ability to speak," Kradik's voice shook, "I would fall dead on the spot before the words escaped my lips."

Dak opened his eyes partway, hoping.

"The spell had a strange effect on our bodies as well," Kradik continued. "Did you know we once had opaque skin like the humans'?" He looked down to inspect his own gloved fingers. "Not as pink or dull as theirs. It sparkled like dew over a sea of flower petals. We were beautiful." He took a deep breath. "But once the spell took effect, our skin changed with it. We've spent several years searching for the escape from this curse."

Curse, Indeed, Dak thought. You brought this on yourselves.

"After many years of investigation, my apprentice, Ortym, and I have learned that a dragon must speak to a human to break this curse."

Is this what they want of me? Dak wondered.

"Don't you see, dragon?" Kradik crouched to look in his eye. "You can save more than just yourself. Say a single word to the humans to break this curse and we will happily release you."

After the lies you've just drooled all over me? Dak thought. I didn't hatch yesterday.

"Ponder your role here, dragon." Kradik stood. "Save yourself and free the faeries, or die a senseless death only to give another dragon the glory of breaking this curse."

As Kradik swept out of the courtyard, Ashel's words finally began to quiet down in Dak's mind. The only question remained, did these two faeries work alone or were other faeries also involved in this betrayal?

Night after night the two faeries returned to beg, plead, threaten, curse and talk until their voices ran hoarse. They did not harm him physically, but their words did him more torment than the humans' sticks or rocks.

These temptations haunted Dak the most. His conscious and his instinct had many silent wrestling matches. The young King Philip seemed like a smart man. He was obviously trying to be a good leader. Dak had seen how angry he had been when his captain got injured. Maybe the humans could care for each other. He might have even seen a glimmer of frustration with the faeries proving the young royal a somewhat logical human. Perhaps he should try to reason with the young man. After all, he wasn't yet a fully grown human. Perhaps his way of thinking wasn't as barbaric as the adult humans.

But no. He had failed the Krusible numerous times. Now that he was on the surface world, he saw the point to it all. The words of his father echoed in his mind through the long days and nights of torture.

"There is a reason for every action. A purpose to every word." He had said with his dying breath. "Try to understand why I have taught you the things I did and you will understand me." Dak more than understood now. Being on the surface was dangerous. A dragon must be prepared to suffer mistreatment. Not only be prepared, but willing to suffer it in silence. Milah's sneering voice was meaningless now. As he got batted around the ears by a gangly old man, he realized he would give anything to see Mitashio over the talon-shaped battlements.

One day the human Jarek came by in the crowd of Dak's tormentors. While the humans on either side of him kicked Dak around his head and neck, Jarek made no move to touch him. He shambled by with his hands shoved deep into the sides of his breeches, but he seemed unable to pry his eyes away from Dak. Dak flinched as the man behind Jarek landed a blow in his eye, but when Dak looked back, Jarek was gone.

My father tried to teach me of the abuse I might be given so I would be strong enough to withstand it and keep this secret intact, Dak thought many times through those weeks. Several times he wept inwardly, but never shed a tear on the outside.

I will suffer my death in silence, he swore an oath to himself, to prove to myself I am worthy to join my father and mother in the World of Souls. Whether my soul is allowed to join them or not, at least I shall depart this life worthy.

After he promised himself this, his yoke eased. Whether by the will of the gods or his strength waning, the guards began to lose interest in him and the flow of humans through the courtyard slowed. The faeries' whispers, however, grew stronger.

"We'll cut you into pieces before we allow you to die," they vowed, reciting details of the parts they would harvest and in what order. "We're very good at our craft. Your soul will never move on to the next world. You'll be trapped as a demon dragon between worlds."

"Loose your tongue and we'll loose your chains," they promised in vain.

But none of their threats could take hold on Dak any longer. The snow fell five different times while he lay in the courtyard. Eventually, it stopped melting except for directly on top of the dragon. His fire burned so low he doubted he could even whisper, let alone speak to save himself.

No. Priya was lost and so was he. He had promised Tog and, in turn, Rakgar, that he would die trying to find her and so he shall. He prayed to the gods that Tog would locate the lost princess and return with her to the Rock Clouds. Perhaps the human he had followed from the mountain knew nothing of the fight. Whatever the meaning of all this mess had been, it would soon be forgotten to Dakoon Ido Tusten. He might not ever join his parents in the World of Souls. He might be doomed to spend eternity tormenting others with no memory of himself, but at least he would leave this life knowing he could still hold his horns high. He was no traitor to dragons. He would be no traitor to himself.

That night as Dak drifted off to sleep, his body ached from the mistreatment. Small cuts and bruises speckled his hide, especially around his head and face. He had worn a depression into the ground beneath him, but as the sun grew colder the mud under his belly began to harden again without his warmth. He rarely tried to lift his head anymore. He could feel his fire going out.

Suddenly a sharp wind blew through the courtyard carrying a familiar scent. Dak recognized it immediately. The odor from human men was of sweat and dirt, but this scent was sweet and more watered down. He lifted his eyelids enough to gaze around in the gathering darkness.

At first he saw only four human guards. Their numbers had dwindled over time. Then he looked into the shadows of the walkway surrounding the courtyard. Standing next to one of the columns was a woman he recognized. He wondered if he had passed into the World of Souls without the humans' knowledge. This was surely the soul of the woman who had come to him in the Black Forest.

Then the fog lifted from his mind and he realized it was the woman he had followed from the fight in the mountains. The woman upon whom he had thrown all his hopes of finding Priya. The woman he had risked everything to hunt down. Princess Anna.

She wore a long silken gown of dark purple. Over it she had a dark cloak with the hood covering most of her golden hair. As he stared at her, she stared back. She never blinked at his gaze.

Brave woman, he thought. Or foolish.

She returned almost every night to the shadows of the covered walkway surrounding the courtyard where Dak was chained. Sometimes she only stayed for a few moments. Sometimes she would stay half the night. But she never approached him. She never spoke to him or threw anything but daggered eyes at him. She never spoke to the guards or anyone else. She just stood in the shadows and watched him. Whatever her role in this tragedy, Dak assumed he would never know.

24

Defense

Philip sat at the writing desk in his office with a small fire crackling in the grate. He had decided to keep the secondary office he had used as a prince rather than move into the king's office. The offices were similar in size and resources, but Philip's was located between the king's office and the castle access doors. He was certain the kings of the past saw this as a safety measure, but Philip only saw it as an inconvenience. So, instead, he assigned the king's office to Torgon. With an adjoining door between the two offices, they could speak to each other whenever they needed without observing formalities.

Today he read over the list of kings and nobles who had written letters with many promises to visit and swear their fealty. Three kings of the Five Swords of Avonoa had promised such, but the one closest to his kingdom had yet to do so. King Theodor – of the Kingdom of the Red Sword of Honor, also known as the Honorable Kingdom – had yet to respond to Philip's ascension. This meant one of two things in Philip's mind: either something had gone wrong in his kingdom, or he disapproved of Philip and planned to petition the other kingdoms for their support in unseating him.

King Theodor of the Honorable Kingdom was older than Philip's departed father, but they had always shared good relations between their two kingdoms. Philip hoped this wouldn't change. Yes, Theodor had always been a coarse man, but he was honorable.

Philip set down the latest letter from King Grisivere of the Just Kingdom when he heard a gentle rap on the door. "Come in."

"Philip." Anna entered, but twisted her hands after she closed the door behind her. She had stopped wearing black following the traditional seven days of mourning – in honor of the seven major gods – but she chose to continue wearing a black veil on her head as was optional for extreme mourning. With it folded back to show her face, Philip could see the red around her beautiful green eyes had eased, but she now showed signs of fatigue in the form of shadows. "This needs to stop," she told him.

"To what are you referring, Anna?"

"The dragon." She pointed in the direction of the courtyard. "This insanity has gone on long enough."

His questioning eyebrows puckered at her words. "What do you mean?"

"Your treatment of that creature." She put her fists on her hips. "You're acting like a spoiled child who's captured an innocent insect."

"Innocent?" Philip stood to look at his sister. "Innocent? That monster slaughtered thirty of my best men along with a man who was like a father to me!"

"What you're doing to him is needless cruelty. He's just a simple animal. He acts on instinct to protect himself."

"Instinct didn't lead him to haunt this land in past weeks, growing closer to Kingstor every moment." Philip lifted several papers from the corner of his massive desk. "Instinct didn't lead him to stalk a Hamees village beyond the pass, or frighten a farmer's wife, or lay in wait in the forest in front of the castle. Do those sound like the actions of a simple animal?"

"What are you saying?" she asked, taken aback. "Are you suggesting this beast did those things with a purpose? That it can think?"

"I'm suggesting nothing." He sat back down behind his desk. "I only know this dragon behaves differently than any other. The faeries warned me of the dragon's odd behavior. Now that I have it, I'll put a stop to its threats."

Anna leaned over Philip's desk. "But does this warrant killing it?"

"Although you've been trained as a noble, Anna," he said, "you have no practical experience." He looked up to meet her eyes. "I must answer to widows and frightened children. You, of all people, should understand the impact a single dragon can have on many lives."

Anna stood to her full height. "Time has taught me to forgive."

"I wish I had that luxury."

Anna turned on her heel to yank the door open, but Philip spoke to stop her. "The guards found your lost maid," he said, without meeting her eye.

"And?" she asked.

Philip hesitated, wondering how harsh he should be. He wasn't sure how much Anna could handle. When she turned a piercing eye on him, he decided bluntness would serve best. "She was killed by a dragon."

"Then it's my own fault for not having sent her with my necklace."

As Anna whipped out the door, Philip's narrowed eyes watched her go. He wondered how a woman who had lost so much at the hands of a dragon could actually be defending one.

25

Deliberate

$\mathcal{S}$now fell on the castle, the tall towers and all around the courtyard repeatedly over the next several days. Sometimes it would melt away during the day to form slick icicles in the night. Sometimes the snow would stay for days at a time freezing the world in a perpetual state of torture.

Eventually the day came when a sudden shiver shook the mighty black beast in his chains. Dak had felt small shivers before, but they weren't a common occurrence for dragons. Many dragons believed it to be a warning of evil nearby. Dak had never heeded the old superstition. In this case, he knew the cold had finally penetrated his hide, meaning his fire was no longer sufficient to warm him. A few minutes later, the king accompanied his faerie allies to visit his captive. They approached the weakened beast across the crusted snow in the courtyard.

"His fire grows weak, Your Highness." Kradik said. "See how the snow stays next to his body without melting. Soon his internal fire will flare to consume his body." The three stood close to the dragon, but still safely to his side despite their knowledge that he could no longer produce flame.

"Is there any way to know for sure?" The young king searched Dak's eyes for any remaining fighting spirit.

"We can test this now," Ortym said as he pulled a dagger from within his cloak. The edges of the blade shimmered as if it had been left to freeze in the snow. Dak recognized the sign of enchantment.

"What will you do with that?" Philip asked.

Kradik withdrew a thick piece of tree bark. On it rested a simple gray rock. "A dragon's blood works like acid on almost everything. Depending on how quickly the rock liquefies, we can tell how long it will take his fire to kill him."

"Stand back," Ortym said as he brought the dagger to Dak's neck. Lifting his hand, he whispered, loud enough for the king to hear, "Tell us your secret, dragon." He continued whispering in an ancient language as he pressed the point of the knife into Dak's neck. The small prick of pain made it difficult for Dak to focus, but he knew he heard the words "sambe" and "kinitar", meaning "blood" and "continue." Dak's heart broke as he realized these faeries knew exactly how to make his blood and body continue long after his soul left them. His soul would never be free.

The long blade slid under his scales, wrenching his mind back to the current threat. Dak couldn't turn his head to see what they were doing and at first he didn't feel anything. But as his hide separated to bare the muscle in his neck, the icy pain cut into him. He thrashed and shook at his bonds, but it offered no relief. He growled at his captors, but the chains encompassing his mouth kept him from roaring properly at them.

The pain subsided quickly enough with no fire to encourage him. He hadn't time to dwell on it before the two faeries stood up to hover over their prize.

"Two days," whispered Kradik.

"No, three," corrected Ortym. Both of the faeries' eyes riveted on a glob of red blood covering the rock. Dak briefly noticed that the bark didn't even seem warm to their gloved hands. It must have been majik-ally reinforced in preparation.

"Three days?" the king asked, but was silenced immediately.

"Shush!" both faeries admonished at once.

"Four, no, five," Kradik said.

"Six."

"Seven."

A burst of steam issued from the spot of blood. Dak thought the two faeries seemed extremely practiced in the art of torturing dragons.

"Eight!" Ortym shouted before the specimen began to boil.

The two faeries straightened from their view of the blood. "Eight days," Kradik answered the king before he dared ask again. "This dragon's blood is powerful," his face twitched toward Dak. "Very powerful. Especially considering the winter cold. In eight days' time this dragon's fire will consume him. In seven days we will harvest and you will be able to take your vengeance, Good King."

King Philip resumed his royal attitude. "Very well." He nodded to the two. "On the morning of the seventh day you can begin your harvest. At midday," he turned back to look at Dak, "I will mount his head on my castle gate."

Dak held still. He only had seven sun-cycles to live. Might as well make the most of it. While the three discussed the parts they would take from him before they killed him publicly, Dak waited. Once their focus left him, he suddenly lurched against his chains with a loud snarl.

He had barely moved, but the unexpected motion made the three men jump. Kradik jolted the boiling substance in his gloved hand. Before he could recover, the acidic blood splashed into the cowl of his cloak. An anguished scream tore from his lips. Without thinking, he threw back the hood of his cloak.

The guards nearby gasped at the sight of the faerie. King Philip's eyes widened slightly in surprise, but he respectfully cast them away. Straight, black hair, the color of Dak's own scales, spilled from the faerie's translucent scalp. High cheekbones and slanted brows magnified the dangerous anger in his eyes. His top lip curled back in a snarl, but whether from anger or pain, Dak couldn't be sure. Like a pebble dropped into water, Dak watched as the acidic blood rippled the faerie's skin into the veins and muscle underneath his cheek and jaw. Finally, the spell holding it must have dissipated because the blood turned to ash and fell away. Eventually his companion pulled a small jar of yellow slime from under his cloak to slather it on his companion's face. As they recovered, King Philip's eyes drifted to Dak.

"That almost seemed deliberate," he said.

"You give him credit where none is due, Sire," Kradik sneered while replacing his cowl. "Else why should he be here?"

The king stood straight then turned his back on the beast. "Why, indeed?" he whispered, more to himself.

———

No closer to finding Priya. Possibly further. Tog nowhere near. Though even if he was, he couldn't do anything. His father dead. His own fire heating his body to self-consumption. If he didn't eat soon, he would be dead in less than a week. Another shiver made his limbs tremble.

Why did I ever leave the Rock Clouds? Dak berated himself. My father, Rakgar, Priya, Tog, even Ashel – they all wanted what was best for me, but I was too stubborn to realize it. If the gods should see fit to spare me, he thought without much hope, they only allow me to go home and die with honor. Even this I don't deserve.

The next sun cycles blurred together. Dak could hardly stay conscious and aware of what was happening around him. One morning, a young boy rolled a long blue cloth on the ground directly in front of Dak. Later some men brought ornate chairs to set them on top of it. Someone added blue drapings on either side of the chairs, decorated with gold and silver symbols of the sun, clouds, moons, stars, trees and animals. The symbols of the gods.

Fewer humans converged on him. Only two guards remained to watch over their prisoner. The guards changed at night, but they usually slept through their watch. Everyone believed the dragon too weak to escape or cause any harm.

Princess Anna's vigils, however, lengthened. Countless hours she stood in the shadows watching the prisoner's slow death. She walked past him in the day as well. Dak wondered if it were possible she knew where he came from.

One day, before the sun went down, a shrill noise blew from the tops of the walls around him.

Is this meant to be more torment for me? Dak wondered. Because it is.

Although his eyes fluttered open for a moment, he couldn't keep their lids aloft long. They fell again as more instruments sounded. Then the trumpeting ceased and the shouting began.

"Hear Ye All!" a voice echoed from the top of the wall. Dak figured the crier must be addressing anyone listening well beyond the castle courtyard. "King Philip of the Noble Kingdom of the Five Swords of Avonoa wishes to send forth a proclamation! Hear Ye All!"

Dak heard murmurs and commotion outside the walls after the voice stopped. Then he heard action high over his head. He lifted his eyes to see King Philip, dressed in royal blue, step onto the balcony to overlook the courtyard and beyond the walls. Before the king noticed him, Dak dropped his eyelids again.

"Good people of the Noble Kingdom," King Philip began, "the day of my coronation draws nigh. As a new king, I wish to make a vow of protection to my people. In the courtyard of the keep, we hold prisoner a black dragon who recently haunted this land and our people. On the morrow, I will prove to you my worthiness to protect the Noble Kingdom, as well as make a belated show of celebration for my sister, Princess Anna. Tomorrow, after my coronation, I will wield the Blue Sword of Nobility and shear off the head of the black dragon. As vengeance for our fathers and brothers it slew, we shall dance around its cold body to prove the strength of humans in the Noble Kingdom!"

His last words drowned in a sea of cheers from the humans outside the wall. Dak listened to the shouts as the king waved to his people then slipped back into his mighty castle.

Die here or at home, he thought. What difference does it make anymore? Dak shivered again in his bonds.

———

The moons had not yet set when Dak roused to the familiar scent of Princess Anna. She wasn't yet in the courtyard, but in the open-air hall on the far side. Next to her a smaller young woman with muddy brown hair stared at the ground. Dak had seen this woman before. She was dressed more like the villager women than royalty.

Anna whispered softly with the smaller woman. The two whispered back and forth to each other. The smaller woman bent to Anna slightly then they both turned to walk into the courtyard.

For the first time Anna refused to meet Dak's eyes as she strolled past in front of him. The smaller woman stopped to make conversation with the first guard. She had a pleasant face and the guard readily smiled back.

Princess Anna, however, continued past Dak to the other guard. Before she spoke she produced a thick fur from under her own heavy cloak. Dak allowed his lids to slip down again, but listened carefully to every sound.

"Good morning, sir," the princess greeted the guard.

"G' mornin', Princess."

"It's a cold morning."

"Right bit'r, Your Highness."

"I brought you an extra cloak."

"Very thoughtful of you, Princess."

Dak lifted one eyelid briefly to see Anna throw the heavy fur over the man's shoulders.

"Is the king forbidding anyone to get near the beast?"

"Yes, My Lady. He was particular 'bout it this mornin'."

The sound of rustling cloth made Dak think Princess Anna remained in physical contact with the guard after giving him the wrapping.

"Surely he doesn't mean to keep me away. I'm the Princess, after all."

"Orders I was gi'en was to keep everyone away 'til the King hisself arrives."

"I just want a little peek." More rustling cloth. "I've always wondered what dragon scales felt like."

The guard gasped. "You mean t' touch it, My Lady?"

"I won't harm it. What could I do to it?"

Silence.

"Please?" she pleaded. "Just for a moment?"

After more hesitation, the man relented. "I'm sure the king didn't mean you to stay away, Princess."

"Exactly. You know your duties well." Dak could feel her eyes turn onto him. "I'll only be a moment."

"Mind you, don' step in fron' of his nose, Princess."

The smell of the woman made Dak's fire grow stronger. In his present state, however, that only meant it would consume him faster. She stepped up to the side furthest from his bound claws. With deliberate movements, she reached an unsteady hand out to the side of Dak's head. Her hand was warm and soft, like the warm breath of a memory brushing the spine in front of his ear. She threw a frail smile to the guard as he watched her. Then slowly she stroked down Dak's long neck.

"Dragon," she breathed the words so low the guards would never hear, but the sound of her voice addressing him brought Dak's eyelids almost completely open. "I know you can hear me," she paused and swallowed, "and I know you can understand me." Her lips barely parted as she spoke.

"You know my scent, I'm sure. You must have followed me here from the mountains. For that, I am truly sorry." She circled slowly around Dak's back. With his sensitive hearing, he caught every word. "Yes, I was there, but I tried to stop the attack. Obviously, I was unsuccessful." She stopped and feigned interest in his tail. "This is all my fault. So I am here to make amends."

When she crossed to the other side of Dak, he noticed the smaller woman throw a furtive glance to the princess as she continued her message. "I've taken the key to your chains from the guard and I mean to free you."

That's all well, thought Dak hopelessly, but I have no strength to flee.

"I ask one small favor in return."

Only one? thought Dak. Why not ask me to carry you away or kill all your enemies for any use I am to you now.

Princess Anna paused as she passed his chains to slide her hand up his neck again. "If you're freed while I'm standing next to you, the king will know I did it and have my head instead." She smoothed one horn on the top of his head then paced back the way she had come. "My maid will distract the guard now while I unlock you, but I beg you to wait until I am gone before you escape." She came to his legs and bent over them for a closer look. "When I'm safely away in my room where no one can claim I've helped you, my maid will appear in the hallway." She looked up casually to inspect the ridges along his spine then bent back down to his claws. "As soon as you see her, muster your strength." She shuddered as she pulled cold air into her lungs. "I cannot watch you die."

The maid giggled out loud in front of the guard as a metallic click sounded between Dak's claws. Princess Anna stopped breathing. Dak realized he was free. He could tear away the chains and fly! But he thought of the sacrifice Anna was making for him – the same sacrifice his father had been willing to make – her life. Dak had failed every other living being in his life. He could not fail the one left that would help him now, even if she was a human.

He felt the lock fall to the frozen mud under his wrist joint. As Anna stood from her supposed inspection with a blank face, he allowed his claw to fall on top of the open lock, hiding it. She inhaled another shaky breath then swept around behind him again.

"Thank you," she whispered as she moved up his back again. Before leaving, she paused by his ear. "The green dragon is in the forest behind the castle. I think she's injured. Save her if you can."

Anna spoke to the guard on her way out, thanking him and whispering conspiratorially as she slipped the key back on his belt. But Dak couldn't focus on her conversation. Priya was alive! Dak tried to calm his burning heart that he might live long enough to save her. She was within his reach! He could not fail her again!

26

Control

The sun had brightened the sky by the time Anna finished her one-sided conversation. As Dak watched, she gathered the maid from her post while King Philip approached from down the hall with the two faerie sorcerers in tow.

"Princess," the king nodded to her as he passed.

"Your Majesty," she nodded back with no stray warmth in her eye. She tried to move past him but he clasped her arm, spinning her to face him.

"Aren't you staying for the celebration?" he motioned to the chairs facing Dak. His words sounded polite, but his tone was accusatory.

"You know how I feel about these proceedings." Her full lips thinned in frustration. "I will, of course, attend the coronation, but you'll have to forgive me a weak stomach for…everything else."

"But this occasion also celebrates your return," he insisted, tightening his hand on her arm. She was taller and older, but he carried a presence to make anyone cower.

"Don't fool yourself. This is a symbol for your reign and nothing more." She looked at the faeries approaching Dak. "What are they doing?" she asked, jabbing her chin in their direction.

Dak watched from the corner of one eye as the faeries took several bottles of different shapes and sizes from under their cloaks.

"Nothing," King Philip shrugged. "They insist on harvesting a few claws in case something goes wrong with their spell that's supposed to keep him from turning to ash."

Anna's jaw clenched. She stared at Dak moving her head ever so minutely from side to side.

Ortym moved closer to whisper more entreaties to Dak. "Speak to the humans, mighty dragon, and we'll not harm a single scale."

Kradik pulled out another long dagger, brandishing it where Dak could appreciate it. The majikal edge shimmered in the winter sun. "Beg for mercy, you worthless snake," he hissed.

"Let me go!" Anna, far enough away not to hear the faeries' voices, pulled against Philip's firm grip. "I can't watch this."

The blade hung over the smallest talon of Dak's left front claw. "Curse us into eternity for all to hear, monster." Ortym's smile was evident in his voice as he placed a conical jar in the snow.

"What would you have me do?" King Philip asked his sister in a low voice. "You're meant to be here."

"No?" Kradik said. "Let's see if this will loose your tongue."

With the least pressure possible, the blade sliced into the flesh of Dak's claw. The cold flowed into the wound encompassing his talon like a ring of ice before it seared through his entire claw and up his foreleg. Forcing himself to keep his back claw over the lock on the ground, the rest of his body writhed in its bonds. He had to fight against the will to lash out at his torturers. His eyes rolled back in his head. His tail thrashed a frenzy in its confines. Feeling as though his fire burned in his belly again, he roared through his muzzle, hoping to alleviate the pain but maintain control of his limbs.

Gaining enough control to open his eyes again, he saw the faeries admiring their acquisition. A single talon floated in a mist of red in the jar they held between them. The stub didn't bleed long, but the faeries salvaged every drop. The pain ebbed back down his leg as Dak's acidic blood sealed the wound's edges, but his claw continued to convulse.

When he could breathe again, Dak's eyes met Anna's. The king had turned to watch him when the dragon roared. Anna's brow compressed on itself. "I'm sorry," she mouthed to Dak behind the king's back.

"Please," she repeated out loud to King Philip. "Please, let me go."

He turned his attention back to her. Seeing her chin tremble and water tumble down her cheeks influenced him. He nodded with resignation and sighed, "I'll make your excuses." Releasing her arm, he said, "Go to your chambers and rest. I'll tell the court you're not well."

Once she was free, Anna quickly gathered her wits. "Thank you, Philip." She bowed deeply before she rushed away.

Dak thought he had never been happier to see a human leave. The faeries gloated over their prize when the king joined them. As he stepped nearer, Dak felt an invisible force, as if a strong wind blew on only him. When he inspected the young king further, he saw a sword hanging at his side from an ornately decorated loop instead of a sheath in order to show off the phosphorescent blue blade like the bracing winter sky overhead.

"Is the spell going to work?" Philip asked the faeries.

They answered in the affirmative just as trumpets sounded and the gates behind Dak opened. King Philip looked to see the addition to the party.

Another human entered Dak's peripheral vision along with several men on horseback. Immediately, Dak felt the pressure of another invisible force from the red sword that flashed at his side. Dak had learned of the majikal swords as a fledgling, but never imagined he would see them with his own eyes.

Within the five different human kingdoms of the Five Swords of Avonoa, each king retained a sword imbued with faerie majik. The faeries had given them to the humans as gifts to help bring – and maintain – peace many millennia ago. The five swords were The Blue Sword of Nobility, The Red Sword of Honor, The Black Sword of Justice, The Silver Sword of Allegiance and The Golden Sword of Courage. The owners of the five swords, the kings of Avonoa, stood as allies and thus never felt the mysterious force from their majikal weapons. But any enemy who found themselves near the swords could sense their power, as Dak could in this moment. The swords gave their users more strength in combat, more swiftness in pursuit and more of the virtue they stood for. Dak thought the kings usually held the swords under protection in their own kingdoms except in times of war.

"King Theodor!" King Philip exclaimed as the older royal approached.

"I came as soon as I heard the news," King Theodor said, dismounting his horse. "I was so sorry to hear about your father, Philip. I hope I haven't missed your coronation."

Philip shook his head. "The coronation is today at midday. Thank you for coming, my friend."

Dak watched King Philip embrace the other king, who was much older than him, but almost a head shorter. His royal garments were similar to Philip's, except his cloak and tunic with the sword across the front were red instead of blue. Theodor had short brown and white hair on his head and chin and he brought with him a dozen more men on horseback with the same red insignia. Dak surveyed the swords at the two kings' sides closer.

The Red Sword of Honor and The Blue Sword of Nobility together at the same time? he wondered. Am I such a threat they feel the need to join these two powerful swords against me?

"Let's take another one," Ortym's voice interrupted Dak's pondering.

Without another thought of the swords, Dak's eyes snapped to the hall where Anna and her maid had disappeared. Just as the dagger pressed into the next talon in line, Anna's maid ran into the hall. She stopped long enough to make eye contact with Dak, who knew his time had come.

The blade cut a gash into his talon before Dak ripped into the dirt under him to avoid it. He swiped his claws back and forth at the faeries as he pulled the chains free.

"What did you do?!" Philip shouted at the faeries, leaving his royal guest's side.

The chains fell from Dak's claws, but he staggered on weakened legs that wouldn't obey his commands. He reached to his head and tore one of the stakes from the ground with his claw, releasing the other stake with the same momentum. He fought with the contraction of his own muscles as well as the chains assailing him.

But he was no longer bound in place. Dak stumbled around the courtyard, tearing at the chains and everyone and everything around him. He could barely get his eyes to focus, let alone make his muscles comply.

Get to the horses! he urged himself. Get to the horses!

Of course the creatures had sensed their danger, but luckily for Dak, their riders hadn't. They forced the beasts to remain in the courtyard as they wielded their swords at the black dragon.

"Secure the chains!" the king shouted to anyone who could comply. "Bind him!"

Dak knew it would be an equal fight in his weakened state against the humans, but that would change if he could get to the horses. Rather than waste his energy trying to free himself from the chains, he floundered across the ground, dragging the binding that still held one leg.

One of the men on horseback stabbed his sword when Dak swayed toward him. Dak swung his head to avoid it, but both beings forgot the two heavy chains draping from his neck. The dirty stakes dangling from the end of the chains struck the man from his beast. After Dak recovered from the surprise of luck, he lunged at the horse's back end – jaws gaping.

"No!" the faeries screamed together.

"Stop him!" the king ranted.

But too late. Dak easily ripped a mouthful of meat from the horse's hind quarter and swallowed. Dak was ravenous for more, but the men behind him continued pulling at the chains or hacking at his scales with their swords. Fortunately, the sustenance the horse provided had eased the debilitating contortions of his muscles. Dak's fire drained from his limbs into his belly and gave him a glimmer of strength.

"The wings!" Kradik yelled. "Sever the wings!"

That won't do at all. Dak decided.

As the men lunged with their weapons toward his wing membranes, Dak pulled himself free of most of his chains. Tucking his wings against him for protection, he reeled his tail and claws in every direction. Men flew against the columns of the yard. Once he had cleared some space, he climbed one of the columns toward the narrow stone walkway atop it.

"Bring it down!" King Philip screamed in rage. "Kill it!"

Dak turned long enough to see King Philip grab a bow and arrow from one of the men now pouring into the courtyard. With a practiced hand, the young king nocked the arrow and let fly. The arrow whizzed past Dak's head close enough to leave a red ribbon on his snout.

Dak didn't wait for the rest of the arrows, spears and even swords being thrown at him. He saw the forest beyond the castle on the other side of the pointed crenelation barring his way. He crawled along the stonework feeling an occasional sting when a sword or arrow found its mark.

For an instant he held a commanding view. Over the castle wall was a sheer drop of many dragon lengths into the forest below. With the recent snowfall tipping the trees, he looked out over a sea of white, gray and green. Dak imagined he saw an opening in the trees not far from the castle's edge. Did he also see a small green lump between the branches? He couldn't be certain.

He tried to climb over the pointed stones, but his claws slipped. Struggling with the almost impenetrable battlements, the rooftop beneath him buckled under his weight for a moment. Just as he bunched his legs and set himself to spring off, something tugged on his tail, holding him down. Dak swung around to face the guard he had recently seen speaking with Princess Anna.

He pulled his tail and the guard in front of him and swiped his claws across the man's face and chest … once … twice. The guard fell to the ground.

"Stop him!" screamed the hapless king.

Both faeries took to the air, but Dak knew of their treachery. One flew in front of him with his fist out. Palm up. Dak knew the toxic dust was clenched in his fingers. Holding his breath to ensure he wouldn't inhale, Dak swiped both front claws at the faerie. They found their marks. The faerie screamed, falling over the steep castle ledge.

"Ortym!" the other faerie yelled.

As Kradik flew to his companion's aid, Dak kicked him with his back leg, sending him reeling into the frozen muddy depression he had left in the brown grass. Kicking at the faerie forced Dak to lean his weight onto one of the pointed stone works. Unable to bear the abuse, the piece gave a loud grating sound before it fell away beneath him. Losing his balance, Dak toppled into the air, unwillingly following Ortym's descent. He thought for a moment, he might be weak enough to die if he hit the bottom. But as soon as he spread his wings, they caught the rushing air. He was free!

27

Hero

Dak let out a mighty roar, the most triumphant he had ever sounded. He glanced back at the castle as he passed the tower where Anna had been heading. Unsurprisingly, he thought he caught the bittersweet sight of a woman's silhouette on the gossamer hangings at the window.

Arrows swiped past him, but after a moment they died away. He swept over the trees then circled the open area he had seen from above. As he flew lower, he saw the distinct shape of a small green dragon. He could have clawed out his own night-blind eyes for the use they had been to him. He had flown over this very spot, weeks ago, and had never seen her in the darkness.

Priya lay unconscious in a swath of white snow. The towering pines nearby kept her concealed. Dak didn't dare call out to her so close to the humans. He didn't want to land, either, for fear he would never get into the sky again. So he hovered over her for a moment before gathering his strength and gently plucking her off the ground.

Her weight threatened to pull them both to the ground. Looking down at her limp, helpless body, Dak knew if he didn't rescue her now, the humans would capture and torture her the same way they had him. He couldn't allow her to suffer that fate! His anger stoked his fire and burned it deep into his belly as well as his chest, head, legs and tail.

He flew away from the king's forest with Priya just above the trees. He would dust the snow from her snout when he had a moment to stop.

Dak knew he needed another helping of meat and remembered the farms near the edge of the wall around Kingstor. Dropping into one of the fields, he left Priya momentarily to crawl to one of the barns. The first animals he saw were small fluffy lumps. He wanted something larger, but they would have to do.

He didn't have much fire, perhaps only one short burst. The little creatures tried to run, but had nowhere to go. When they cowered against the far wall, Dak shot them with what little fire he could spare. Most of them scurried out of the way, but three were not so fortunate. When the fire burned away he saw that their bodies were not as big as he had hoped, but it would be enough to get him away from Kingstor with Priya.

As Dak dug into his first charred bites, a woman came from the building adjacent to the paddock. She and Dak stared at each other and for a moment Dak thought she might actually fight him for the prize he devoured. But when he gave her a low menacing growl, she screamed and ran away.

Great, he thought, no time to enjoy my meal before the humans multiply again.

Finishing off the first morsel quickly, Dak scooped up the other two in one claw and ran back to Priya. He had hoped she would wake while he was gone, but she lay motionless in the same place he'd left her.

He nudged her with his nose and waited for a response before he shoved her with his shoulder. Nothing. Then, slumping to the ground, he ate another of the little creatures while watching over her.

"Priya," Dak whispered when only one animal remained. If Rakgar's daughter needed the food more than he did when she awoke, he didn't want to be responsible for her starvation. "Priya!" he whispered again, a little harsher. Still nothing.

He couldn't wait much longer. Dak knew humans would soon swarm this area in search of him. He had to leave with Priya now. Scanning the landscape around them, Dak got his bearings and quickly planned his route back to the Rock Clouds. He ate the last beast in a few bites, cradled his princess again and took to the skies.

He flew through the mountain pass where he had followed Princess Anna, then past the little community where she had stayed. He headed into the mountains to the scene of the initial attack on the dragons. Dak's strength flowed strong though him. His body wouldn't be completely healed for a few days, possibly longer, but at least he could easily carry Priya now.

He landed on one of the mountain's rocky projections to search for traces of recent dragon visits, but found none. Had it really been long enough to erase all clues of Tog and the fresh contingent? Or had they even come?

Instead of flying on, Dak decided to rest where the mountains met the Black Forest. He knew it would take the humans several sun cycles to reach this point. If they were still alive, the faeries could only fly as fast as a human could run, but he hoped the two traitors had learned their lesson. He found a small cave on the side of the mountain where he could sleep. He hadn't realized how tired he was until he lay curled up beside Priya somewhere hard and safe.

—

Dak woke to the three moons of Avonoa hanging over the forest in front of him. Priya still lay curled on the stone floor. Breathing softly, she seemed to be sleeping comfortably.

Dak sat up. His body ached. He closed his eyes to take account of his injuries. Two had begun healing, but his tail still had three long open gashes. His wing membrane, usually the first thing to heal on a dragon, only had two small holes left to scab over. Seeing the numerous holes, he wasn't sure how he had flown at all. His head and face had the most damage with cuts and scrapes and the long gash King Philip had left him. His back and belly, which were missing scales and bruised, held numerous cuts in his thick hide. His back two legs were also missing scales, but they would grow back over time and the bruises underneath would heal quickly. His front legs looked as bad as his back... except...

He had been avoiding it, but Dak finally looked down at his left front claw. Only three sharp points remained. He sighed. The scabbed stub had already hardened to seal the edge. The sight of the jagged red stump threatened to rip his heart out. He could imagine Milah's and Mitashio's insults and wondered if he would live long enough to hear them.

He tore his eyes away from his foot to look out over the forest in front of him. He couldn't see much with his poor night vision, but the view of the trees below glazed with fresh snow and moonlight almost made him want to weep. Despite its dangers, the surface world was beautiful. And this might be the last time he would ever see it.

He had flown for three sun cycles to get away from the Rock Clouds, but Dak knew he could retrace his flight in less than two. The contingent hadn't been pressing hard on their initial flight and neither had he. By resting on the mountainside first, he hoped to gather enough strength to avoid landing in the Black Forest at all.

The small meal of the fluffy barn animals had only partially filled his belly, so he would have to watch for another source of food if he was going to press himself harder on the return trip. He wished Priya would wake, but he couldn't spare fire to heal her. Not until he had healed himself.

His eyes wandered over to the sleeping princess, but continued on to something he hadn't seen in the daylight. Indeed, it couldn't be seen in daylight at all. Behind the two dragons grew a small red plant with the appearance of fire frozen in time. Flarote. Named in the Faerie tongue as "burning mushrooms," a single tiny plant could cure almost any creature, even a dying dragon. Flarote usually grew in warm, dark places, which is why the Rock Cloud Ruck took up its home where it did. The little specimen in this cave probably grew plentifully in the summer. It was a miracle one had lasted this long. Dak's heart leapt when he saw it.

He speared the little red bulb with one talon, but before he put it in his mouth he approached Priya. She lay with her mouth closed, breathing hot air softly through her nose. He didn't know how he could make her swallow it, so he decided to eat it himself and heal her with his fire.

Popping it into his mouth, it melted like a soft liver from a freshly hunted lydik and tasted just as good, but it was warm to the point of burning. His father had taught him that eating too many flarote would kill him. This was true with every dragon and they guarded this secret most jealously so as not to reveal their vulnerability. Even the centaurs and faerles didn't know.

Dak felt the single mushroom burn through him and heal the many cuts and bruises all over his body. The scales would grow back more slowly, but with this his body would be able to direct more healing energy into them. He swept his tail around in front of him to watch the gashes close together. With half a hope, he looked down at his left front claw.

No luck. The flarote healed the edge completely, even starting the growth of small scales to cover the edge, but no talon would ever grow in its place. Once a dragon lost a part of himself, he lost it forever.

Turning his attention to his sleeping friend, Dak bathed Priya's still form in fire. For a moment, he wasn't sure it would work. After all, he didn't know what the faeries had done to her or what majik they might have used.

With a gasp and a flutter of her eyelids, Priya stared up at Dak. "Dakoon?" she whispered.

"Yes, Priya," he answered. "You're safe. Do you remember anything?"

"I...we..." she stuttered then gazed up at Dak with wide eyes. "We were attacked. The contingent."

"Yes, I know," he nodded. "What else do you remember?"

"I chased after a faerie to see if I could talk to him, then...then..." she closed her eyes and shook her head. "I don't remember anything else."

"It's ok," he reassured her, "we're safe now."

"What happened to the others?" she asked. Then she looked around. "Where are we?" She looked at Dak through narrowed eyes then jumped to her feet. "What are you doing here, Dakoon?"

"Don't worry," Dak answered. He'd expected her response. "I'll tell you everything."

Slowly, she sat down on the ground in front of him. He decided to tell her, but not necessarily show her everything that had happened. He wasn't sure how much he should tell others of what Anna did for him.

"I followed you," he said.

Priya shook her head. "You witless worm..." Dak allowed her a moment of disdain. He was sure it wouldn't be the last. "What happened to Tog and the rest of the contingent?"

"They're all dead," he whispered, "except for Tog."

She gnashed her teeth as she growled at the moons. Turning back to Dak, she whispered, "Show me."

He wanted to spare her pain, but he couldn't deny her the knowledge of what had happened. Placing his nose in front of hers, he recalled the memories of finding the ember remains of the other dragons and finding his father, then he exhaled. He kept his father's dying words to himself; it seemed they were meant only for him. Then he showed her his heroic rescue of Tog.

When she had seen all the memories she blinked and nodded. "I'm glad Toggil is safe," – tears filled her eyes – "but I'm so sorry about Tusten."

Dak placed one claw on top of hers, "You aren't to blame."

When she gasped in shock, Dak realized he had placed his left claw over hers. "By The One! What happened to your claw?!" she shrieked.

He yanked it away to fold it under his belly, but she narrowed her eyes at him again. "Dakoon Ido Tusten. Tell me all."

With a deep sigh, he faced her again. This time he recalled following the human scent. He showed her his flight chasing Anna to Kingstor. He showed her the faeries tricking him and capturing him. He showed her his slow torture at the hands of the humans. He showed her everything Anna had said and done. Finally, he showed her his escape from the castle and the flight here with her in his arms. It took a few breaths.

When he finished, he waited silently. "Oh, Dakoon," she barely spoke, "what you have suffered!" She shook her head. "Surely my father will see you've borne enough."

"Priya," Dak studied the stone floor. "I'm prepared to accept my punishment."

Both dragons lay their heads down on the cave floor as the moons crossed the sky. After a time, Priya spoke. "Dakoon," she started, "when I was first introduced to the dragons as Rakgar's daughter, no one knew who I was or where I had come from, particularly who my mother was."

Dak looked at her sideways, wondering. "You and Toggil," she continued, "were the first to accept me.

I'm not sure you even thought about your actions at the time. We were only fledglings. But your acceptance led others to accept me." She paused to take a breath. "I can never repay that debt, but I give you my wyrd – "

"No!"

" – that I will speak to Rakgar on your behalf – "

"No!"

" – and bear any punishment with you," she finished.

"Priya, no!" Dak insisted. "Lying there waiting for death to take me, I would have given anything to return to my home to die among dragons. I won't let you throw your life away after I've just saved it!"

Priya laid her head on the ground. "It is done."

"But I release you from your wyrd."

"You cannot release me from this," she mumbled without looking at him.

Dak knew Priya would hold fast to her wyrd, like any dragon. He knew they would return to the Rock Clouds, but now it would be not only his life hanging on Rakgar's judgment.

—

Neither dragon spoke for the remainder of the night. They rested in the warm, dark cave well after the sun rose, but neither slept. Eventually, Dak sat up.

"We need to eat before we press on," he said.

Priya joined him at the cave opening. "The winds are blowing toward the Rock Clouds," she answered. "We can travel with them and find food along the way."

"Are you well enough to fly?"

She nodded. "Are you?"

He nodded back.

Priya jumped into the sky first with Dak close at her tail. Spreading his wings, Dak thought of returning home. For either death or life, there was nowhere else he'd rather be.

The pair flew over the tall frosted trees of the Black Forest. Now in the last month of winter, the sun had begun to burn warmer in the Avonoan sky. Dak closed his eyes for a few moments to enjoy the warmth on his wings and back. He even rolled for a moment to savor the feeling on his belly. He thought he would never feel this good again.

A sharp snap of Priya's jaws forced him to roll upright and look at her.

"Sorry to interrupt," she grinned at him then jerked her head toward the ground. "I thought you might like a last meal."

Below them a frozen river wound around the border of the Black Forest. Beyond that stretched miles of what Dak assumed would be lush green and yellow grasslands in the summer, but now it was a frozen white mass dotted with snow-covered trees. Next to the river by some tall pines, a large herd of lydik dug under the snow for a meal.

The two dragons burst from the sky before the beasts even knew of any danger. They ate an entire lydik each. After their meal they raced each other into the sky again with their bellies burning hot.

The winds did indeed push them toward the Rock Clouds. Perhaps it was the wind or perhaps it was because there were only two of them so they could travel faster, but whatever the reason, the dragons soon landed by the same river where they had spent the first night of their journey, albeit apart.

Dak stared into the darkness on one side. "I was over there," he said.

Priya had collapsed on the rocky bank of the river, but lifted her head to look into the darkness where he indicated. Looking back at Dak she said, "My father will forgive you, Dakoon."

He shook his head slowly. "No," he said as he lay down next to her, "he won't." He placed his nose in front of hers to show her the memory Tog had given him so long ago.

He thought about his father telling Rakgar his son wouldn't flee, then swearing an oath to take his son's punishment alongside him if he did. This memory haunted Dak the most while he suffered at the hands of the humans.

After Priya experienced the memory she said nothing. "Don't worry," Dak told her, "I'm not going to run. Not this time."

Again she said nothing in response, but the question clearly crossed her brow as she narrowed her eyes at him. "I give you my wyrd," he promised. "I would rather die by Rakgar's claw than live the rest of my life as a fugitive on the surface." He laid his head down on his claws then added, "I'm prepared to accept the consequences of my mistakes."

Priya stretched her long neck to search Dak's eyes. He looked back at her, unashamed of his behavior for the first time in his life.

"You really have changed," she whispered to him. "You're no longer just Dakoon. You're..." she paused to think and a grin curved the edges of her mouth. "You're my hero."

28

Acceptance

When Dak awoke the next morning the moons of Avonoa glittered over the trees below while the sun's first rays glowed. Priya sat up staring into the sky as silent as the sun itself. The pair soon sprang into the air and flew for most of the day.

The Rock Clouds had come clearly into view the previous day, but as they flew closer Dak's heart sang with joy. Even with the winter cold, he could see a few dark shapes flying among the drifting masses. Whether he returned to the Rock Clouds to live or die, he would soon be home.

They flew most of the day with the Rock Clouds directly ahead of them. The indistinct masses taking shape before their sharp eyes with every wingfall. The distant sun cast long shadows as they finally neared the outermost floating mountain. Priya swung closer alongside Dak. "Speak to no one," she told him. "Don't even look at them if you can help it. We fly for Rakgar's lair and stop for no other."

Dak nodded. He knew better than to answer her within hearing distance of others. As a criminal in the dragons' eyes, Dak had lost his right to speak to anyone. His only hope for redemption would be to offer Rakgar his memories.

As the two dragons flew past The Watch, the sentries roared challenges. A few left their posts to pursue them, but neither Priya nor Dak glanced their way.

Flying past the floating dragon lairs, Dak could hear whispers and exclamations. He didn't know if Priya heard them; she certainly didn't let on if she did. Many dragons left their dwellings to follow them. As they approached the Inner Mountain, Dak's mountain home also came into view. A jagged hole in the mountainside marked the location from which the balancing rock had been forced from its home. In the soft evening light he could just make out a large gray dragon alight from it to join the throng.

Just before they reached the edge of the Inner Mountain, one of The Watch shot between the two dragons and their goal. Roaring a challenge, he forced them to hover for a moment. In answer, Priya roared while issuing a burst of flame directly at the splotchy brown dragon's face. While he couldn't see her, she flew in closer. When the flame died away from the sentry's eyes, she raked her claws across his face. She refused to be disallowed to see her father.

When they finally landed on the edge of Rakgar's lair, Dak could feel a large fraction of the ruck gathering outside on the feeding grounds to await the decision – and ultimately, the punishment – of the criminal Dakoon.

Their claws clacked on the hard, cold floor as they stepped into Rakgar's hall. Rakgar sat in council with five other dragons. Milah was one of them. Next to him stood a faerie with silver blonde hair. The hood of her cloak hung at her back to reveal her face, unlike the covering that Kradik and Ortym wore in the humans' presence. Her transparent skin could clearly be seen on her hands and head. Dak couldn't help his reaction to seeing one of the beings who had tortured him. He crouched to the ground and growled.

The entire group whipped around at the sound of the newcomers. Milah smirked at Dak before Priya brought him back to his senses with a tail slap on his shoulder.

"Shining days, Dromdan Rakgar," Priya addressed her father.

"Clear skies, Priya," Rakgar said. "I thought you were lost." Dak didn't think his greeting conveyed the warmth she deserved.

"So I was, father."

Rakgar glanced around at the audience. "Please leave us," he told them.

"No," Priya interrupted before they could leave. "I'm here to speak for Dakoon."

"What?" Rakgar growled.

"Your council needs to hear what I have to say."

Rakgar rumbled in the back of his throat again. "Choose your words carefully, young one."

Priya nodded to her father, but her eyes never left his. Behind them, Dak heard another dragon enter the cavern. Glancing back he saw the familiar face of his best friend. They nodded to each other before Dak turned back around to accept his fate.

"The dragon, Dakoon, risked his life to find me." Priya spoke to Rakgar and the council. "He was among the humans for several weeks and he never spoke a word. Even under torture," she eyed the faerie briefly before snatching Dak's claw into the air, "he did not reveal our secret. I believe the dragon who left the Rock Clouds as a criminal no longer exists."

"You know this from speaking with him," Milah protested from Rakgar's side.

"I know this from his actions," Priya insisted. Letting Dak's claw drop again, she turned to her father. "After leaving the Rock Clouds against the law, would the dragon Dakoon have returned to accept his punishment?"

Rakgar paused in thought. For what seemed like forever, he stared at Dak and Priya. "No," he finally answered, "the Dakoon I knew would have run." Dak took a breath. "Nevertheless," Rakgar said, and Dak stopped breathing again, "the law has been broken."

Priya narrowed her eyes and Dak could see her jaw working. "Now," she said through her fangs, "I will speak with you in private."

Rakgar stared at her, but waved his claw for the others to leave. Dak stayed to hear his fate, but Priya turned to him. "You too, Dakoon."

At her insistence Dak joined the throng outside the lair. He moved to one side of the cave while at least fifty other dragons stared at him from the other. He curled up on the ground just as Tog started toward him.

A dragon named Nimas grabbed his back leg to stop him. "Toggil, don't," he said.

Tog jerked his leg free with a low growl. He moved directly in front of Dak. Dak had already decided not to speak to Tog, as much as it might hurt both of them. He didn't want his best friend to suffer alongside him. Not if he could help it.

But Tog didn't speak. He placed his face in front of Dak's and passed a memory to him.

Instantly Dak stood in Rakgar's lair again, but this time he heard Tog's voice.

"Rakgar we must gather a new contingent and search for Priya," Tog said.

"No," Rakgar answered. "It would be too suspect to the humans."

"Then we must go to the faeries," Tog tried again. "Ask them if they know anything. Beg their help."

A faerie materialized from a cavern next to Rakgar.

"I have already spoken to them," Rakgar said. "Priya is lost. You must accept this."

"But Rakgar – " Tog started before he was cut off.

"NO!" Rakgar roared. "That is my final word. You will remain in the Rock Clouds to wait for another assignment." Rakgar took a step closer. "Be grateful I don't punish you for speaking to Dakoon."

Dak blinked back into his own body as Tog turned and walked away. So this was the reason Tog had not returned to the surface. Rakgar had ordered him to abandon his two best friends. Even though he had been through torture with the humans, Dak realized that Tog had suffered just as much torment of his own. Watching the back of his best friend retreat, Dak felt willing to have another talon chopped off if it would take away Tog's pain.

All too soon for Dak, Priya called out to him. He flew back into Rakgar's lair to two very solemn dragons.

"Dakoon," Rakgar said, "give me your memories of your time among the humans."

Dak crawled to Rakgar and breathed into his face. He showed him the remains of the attack on the contingent. He gave him the memories of Jarek and his village. He shared his flight to follow Princess Anna. He showed him the faeries' trickery to capture him. He showed the faeries attempting to harvest him. And he divulged everything Princess Anna had said and done to free him and reveal Priya's whereabouts.

When he finished, Rakgar simply nodded then walked past him to the edge of the cave. Priya gave him a weak grin as they stepped together behind him.

Rakgar roared out the cave's entrance to the dragons waiting outside. "The black dragon Dakoon has passed the Krusible in the most dangerous and important arena of all. He kept his silence on the surface for weeks under torture and near death. I claim he is hereby forgiven of all past infractions of the law by proving himself worthy to hold our secrets. Dakoon Ido Tusten shall be known hereafter as Hiro Tekla."

Dak, now Hiro, swiveled his head around to Priya. "The 'three-clawed hero'," she whispered to him. "I had already renamed you after all."

Hiro couldn't stop himself from returning her smile, but he knew there was one more thing he had to tell Rakgar.

"Rakgar," he said as the leader walked past him back into his cave.

"Yes, Hiro?" he answered. Although he was supposed to act like Hiro was a completely different creature than Dakoon, Hiro couldn't help but notice the impatience in his tone.

"There were two swords at Kingstor," he said.

"I saw that in your memory, Hiro."

"But Rakgar – " Hiro started.

"What humans do with their toys is not our concern," Rakgar interrupted him. "Perhaps, if we're lucky, they'll use them to kill each other off." Rakgar chuckled at the notion.

"But the faeries – " Hiro tried again as the silver-haired creature flew back into the lair.

"You only met two faeries," Rakgar said as the faerie and the rest of Rakgar's council entered the lair to take their places at his side. "I'm sure they worked the sorcery of their own accord."

"Rest assured, mighty Hiro," the faerie hummed as she hovered in front of him. "If there be any faeries who dare plot against our allies the dragons, I shall not rest until they're discovered."

Before Hiro could argue, even though he didn't know what he would say, Tog ran into the cave and thumped him with his tail. The smile on his face drove any thoughts of faerie betrayal from his mind.

As he turned to leave, Rakgar called out to Hiro one last time.

"Should I assume you'd like to be assigned to Priya's contingent?" he asked.

Hiro glanced at Priya and nodded to her before he replied, "As much as I will always be at Priya's service, Rakgar, I have had quite enough time away from my home. I desire nothing more than to remain in the Rock Clouds and share my experiences with hatchlings so they might not suffer as I."

The dragons around him murmured, but Rakgar nodded. "You truly have changed. So be it."

When Hiro turned to leave again he caught site of Tog's drooping eye. "What's wrong?" he asked, surprised at his friend's change in countenance.

Tog shifted his shoulder slightly. "It's all we've ever dreamed of," he said, "going down to the surface together." The hurt in his eyes made Hiro's resolve sway. "Do you really want to give it up?"

"There will be other dreams, my friend," Hiro answered. "Perhaps in time the adventurous spirit will writhe within me again."

"Besides," Priya said, joining the two dans, "he won't be able to see our favorite places unless he comes with us eventually!"

As the three friends ran out the cave entrance, Hiro saw the flash of a white tail in his peripheral vision. "Give me a moment," he said to his friends, but he didn't wait to see their questioning looks before he pursued the last place he might have seen her.

Hiro scrambled up the mountainside outside Rakgar's lair. Just as he thought he might have imagined it, he caught sight of the white dragon climbing toward some frosted pines. He charged after her, keeping the tip of her tail in his line of vision. When he was close enough to be heard, he called out.

"Visi!" he bellowed. The prophetess stopped and turned slowly with knowing eyes, but didn't say a word. "Why?" he asked simply when he stood in front of her.

"Why what?" she growled. "In my line of habit you must be specific in your questions."

"Why did you help me escape? No – " he caught himself in the same breath. Many questions had gone through his mind in the past weeks, questions he thought would never be answered. Now he wasn't sure which one to ask first. "No, my first question is ... why didn't you stop the attack?"

She stared at him in silence.

"You knew the attack was imminent, didn't you?" Hiro questioned his assumption, but only briefly.

Visi dipped her head.

"Why didn't you tell someone? We could have stopped it!" he roared at her. "The lives lost!"

"I considered telling those involved, Hiro," she said, sneering his name, "but none of them would have made the right decision."

"Then someone else, perhaps." He raised his top lip at her. How could she presume to play the role of the gods? "You have an entire ruck at your disposal."

"I do not have the luxury to look into the future of every dragon here, you fool," she said. "It was the necessary outcome for those circumstances. After all, I do not act unless I see my own actions in the futures of others."

"The 'necessary outcome'?" he asked again. "But you could have – "

"If you hadn't left on that rock of yours," she continued over his protests. "You would've been caught and killed!"

Hiro snapped his jaw shut at her words.

"If you had chosen to stay, you would've failed your last Krusible, lost your ability to ever leave the Rock Clouds, tried to escape later and been caught and killed." She stepped closer to him. "I gave you the only option left to gain your freedom and also hear your father's dying words. Now you tell me, would you have had me change my actions?"

Hiro gave his head a small shake.

"Heed your father's words well, Hiro," she said in her choking voice. "Learn to understand before you question. Or you dishonor his memory."

"Hiro!" He turned to look behind him toward the shouts from his two best friends. When he turned back, Visi was gone.

Tog's smile slowly returned as they pushed past the pines. "Hiro," he shook his head, "you were right, you know." Hiro threw him a questioning look. "You found a way!"

Hiro glanced once more at the spot where Visi had stood before the three friends dashed out of the trees and launched into the darkening sky.

—

THE END

Acknowledgments

I would like to thank everyone who has done so much to help me with this project.

Thank you to my editor, Sue Goolsby. Your insight and knowledge was invaluable.

Thank you to my cover artist, Kay Cooper. You made my vision come to life!

Thank you to my map artist, Kathy Morse. Your talent gave me a dragon's eye view!

Thank you to my proofreaders, my dad - Darryl, and my sister - Christi. Your keen eyes were a huge relief when mine went fuzzy from repetition.

Thank you to my readers, my mom - Lyndel, my husband - Jason, and Tamar Neumann. Thanks for sharing in this great adventure with me and Dak!

Also, thanks to the SouthSide Writers for your encouragement and support!

Made in the USA
Lexington, KY
19 August 2018